FADEAWAY

Also by Steven Barwin in
the Lorimer Sports Stories series

Rock Dogs
SK8ER
Icebreaker
Roller Hockey Blues (with Gabriel Tick)
Slam Dunk (with Gabriel Tick)

FADEAWAY

Steven Barwin

with a foreword by Q-Mack

**James Lorimer & Company Ltd., Publishers
Toronto**

James Lorimer & Company Ltd., Publishers acknowledges the support of the Ontario Arts Council. We acknowledge the financial support of the Government of Canada through the Canada Book Fund for our publishing activities. We acknowledge the support of the Canada Council for the Arts for our publishing program. We acknowledge the Government of Ontario through the Ontario Media Development Corporation's Ontario Book Initiative.

Library and Archives Canada Cataloguing in Publication
Barwin, Steven
Fadeaway / by Steven Barwin.

(Sports stories)
Issued also in an electronic format.
ISBN 978-1-55277-547-9 (pbk.). — ISBN 978-1-55277-548-6 (bound)
ISBN 978-1-55277-549-3 (e-book)

I. Title. II. Series: Sports stories (Toronto, Ont.)

PS8553.A7836F34 2010   jC813'.54   C2010-902617-9

James Lorimer & Company Ltd.,   Distributed in the United States by:
Publishers   Orca Book Publishers
317 Adelaide St. West   P.O. Box 468
Suite 1002   Custer, WA USA
Toronto, Ontario, Canada   98240-0468
M5V 1P9
www.lorimer.ca

Printed and bound in Canada.
Manufactured by Webcom in Toronto, Ontario, Canada in August 2010.
Job # 370668

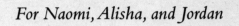

For Naomi, Alisha, and Jordan

CONTENTS

FOREWORD

In my line of work, you get to meet a lot of people. I've had the chance to host events for NBA All-Stars like Steve Nash and LeBron James, interview Shaquille O'Neal, and even perform at Chris Bosh's Christmas party! Every couple of years, I'm introduced to someone who just seems to stick out in my mind. The author of this book you're about to read, my boy Steve Barwin, is one of those people. I met Steve while performing my "bullying themed' basketball trickshow at the school that he teaches at and have kept in contact with him through out the years. When I heard he was writing a book on my two favourite subjects, basketball and bullying, I was instantly intrigued. I was even happier when I read it and realized that he managed to write a real winner here, or as I say "nothin' but NET!!"

I can tell you one thing about Steve. He's not as tall as Shaq, he's not a fast a Nash, and he can't jump as high as LeBron, but my boy's got as much heart as any one of those MVP's! That is the statistical category that isn't measured in the NBA, but this book is all about heart. Trying your best, working hard, and standing up for other people who don't feel strong enough to stand up for themselves. So join Steve as he attempts to "slam dunk" bullying, and remember:

Together We Can Increase the PEACE!!

I hope you enjoy the book as much as I did.

Your Boy,

Q-Mack

1 SWARM OF HORNETS

Through a crowd of yellow and white jerseys, the basketball found my hand. I deflected it down into a shallow dribble. Then I brought the ball to the top of the key, in line with the net, and shouted, "Get open!"

Looking around for someone to pass to, I saw my Hornet centre and best friend, Jessie. She was near the net. I looked to Emma deep in the corner, but the other team covered her worse than bees on honey. Between the arms of the girl covering me I found my shooting guard, Grace. She was small, but under her short black hair is the brain of a math genius. With quick calculation, she could determine the right speed and height to sink a three-pointer from the moon — if she wasn't being covered by someone taller.

The thirty-second shot clock counted down in my head — *ten, nine, eight . . .*

Through the Warrior players I eyed Caitlyn running a sharp *V* on the left side to the baseline. She shot back toward me, losing her cover on the way. I chest-passed the ball hard to her and she caught it running toward me.

Six, five, four . . .

I moved forward, past my cover, and Caitlyn side-passed the ball back to me.

I drove deep into the key, cutting between two Warrior defenders. They tried their best to knock me, the ball, or both of us, down, but I came in with tornado-like speed. They didn't stand a chance. I moved from my right foot to my left foot, grabbed the ball in both hands, and pushed off the ground with my right foot. Soaring up and on an angle, I stretched up my right hand and fed the ball gently against the backboard and into the net — a perfect layup.

Swoosh.

I haven't heard a better sound in my twelve years on this planet. And by this planet, I don't mean I've lived anywhere cool like Paris or Dubai. Just a place called Richmond Hill.

Back on the ground, I turned under the basket and slapped hands with Caitlyn.

"Nice job, quarterback," Caitlyn said.

"Don't you mean point guard?" I asked.

Caitlyn smiled. "Same thing."

On my way back into the Hornet half, I made sure to take a big high-five from Jessie. We've known each other as long as I can remember, since grade one, I'm pretty sure. We were always the only girls in gym class who were happy to be in gym. I remember upsetting the boys by beating them at, well, everything. They'd always try to do stupid boy things like change the rules at the last minute or fake horrible injuries. But in my book, a win is a win.

"Nice bucket," Jessie said.

"Thanks. What's going on with you and that Warrior centre?"

"Just giving me a hard time. She's stronger on her right, so I'm switching to the left side."

"That's playing with your brains."

I refocused on the play when the Warriors turned up their offensive game. They were coming at us fast. "Hands up and take them to the line!" I called. It wasn't a shout or an order, just good communication, helping everyone play a heads-up game.

"Cover Number 11, Renna!"

I spotted Coach Philip pointing with his clipboard from the sidelines. Warrior Number 11 had the ball. She tried to fake me left, right, then left, but I just stood in front of her with my elbows bent and my hands up, blocking her shot, pass, and vision. I had worked too long and too hard this season to give up this game and our first-place position in the league. Coach had wanted one practice a week, but I had convinced him that two were needed.

Number 11 called out angrily to her teammates, "Get open!" I noticed the *C* on her jersey.

A captain should never talk to her team that way. She pivoted around me, clipping my shoulder on the way, and when she passed the ball I managed to get some skin on it. The ball bounced clumsily on the hardwood and reached the shooting guard, who lined up to the net and released a three-point shot. The ball bounced off the rim and landed in the hands of Emma. Before I could say, "Pass to me," I heard Coach shout out, "Time!"

The referee blew his whistle. I noticed Number 11 was reaming out her shooting guard for missing the bucket. I scurried back to the bench in need of a towel and some cold water.

"Gather around, everyone." Coach Philip wiped sweat off his forehead and stared down at his clipboard like it was the source of all magical basketball plays. "Catch your breath, drink some water."

I had Coach Philip as a teacher last year, in grade six. I knew he didn't have the experience the other team's coach had.

Philip continued. "Clock's running down. There's only a minute-twenty left in the game and we're ahead by two."

"So?" I had to ask, as the Hornets captain.

"So, I say we run down the clock."

"We can't do that Coach."

"Well, then, what do you recommend we do?"

I said, "Get an insurance basket," surprised that

everyone else wasn't already thinking that.

"I don't know if that's a good idea."

I watched him look down at his clipboard again. One time at practice I took a peek and saw that he had pages printed off from the Internet on it.

Jessie jumped in. "She's right. One more would guarantee us the win."

"Well, just let me think."

I looked at the other girls while he spent the last ten seconds of the timeout thinking. The buzzer sounded. I still waited for an answer. "Coach?"

"Okay, okay. Go for the insurance bucket."

I hurried back into position and Grace threw the ball in play. I grabbed it and dribbled it into Warrior territory. I needed to create a play. Just past the centre line I bounce-passed the ball to Emma, who took it up the right side and quickly became boxed in. I moved right in front of the player covering Emma and crossed my hands over my chest, dug in my feet, and supplied a block. Emma moved around me. When she found a clearing, I rolled around the defender and took position in the corner. Emma passed the ball to Grace. She didn't have a shot.

"I'm in the open!" I shouted.

Grace passed the ball to me in the corner. I grabbed it and went for the big shot. As the ball sailed through the air, I took a peek at the clock — twenty-five seconds. I couldn't believe my bad luck when the ball hit the rim, bounced off the backboard, and dropped to the ground, missing the net.

Warrior players screamed, "Get the ball."

Every Hornet yelled, "Get back and cover the net!"

I tried to move, but it felt like my feet where glued to the floor. I swallowed the guilt of taking the risky shot and scurried back to help my team. But it was too late. I raced over the centre line as Warrior Number 9 raised the ball for a shot.

She's going for a three-pointer, I thought, *a game winner.*

If I could, I would have reached out to smack the ball away, but she was taller than I am. She released the shot just as the buzzer rang. The ball arched up and toward the net. My stomach seemed to sink down to my knees. I only wished that I had time to pray. I didn't want to watch, but I couldn't look away either.

All I could think was, *Goodbye, first place. Goodbye, league championship. Goodbye, Renna Rashad, captain of the Richmond Hill Losers.*

2 MINUS A HORNET

The ball hit the rim and the vibration sent a ringing sound through my ears. I opened my eyes and looked up, ready to admit that it was my fault we had lost the game.

But the ball bounced off the rim, hit the backboard, and dropped toward the hoop. Out of nowhere, Jessie popped up and, stretching to her full awesome length, swatted the ball away as if it was an annoying bug spoiling a picnic. The ball bounced out of bounds as the final buzzer sounded. No basket! Game over! We won!

Okay, so maybe I was being a little dramatic about the "Richmond Hill Losers." We're a great team with great players. We're the Richmond Hill Hornets, the *first-place* Richmond Hill Hornets.

Coach Philip was the first to shout out, "We won, we won!"

I ran up to Jessie and gave her a big hug. "Thank you, thank you, thank you."

She wore a well-earned, game-saving smile. "No problem. Just doing my job."

"I'm just thanking my stars that you had an early growth spurt."

Jessie didn't know how to take my compliment, so we just high-fived each other and everyone else over and over.

The coach interrupted our celebration. "Now, let's not get big egos. Bring it down and line up for handshakes."

I stepped in line between Caitlyn and Grace as the Warriors passed by with their heads bowed low.

"Good game, good game, good game, good game, good game." By the sixth player my "good game" sounded more like "g-game."

When I reached Number 11, the Warrior point guard and captain, I kept my hand out for a high-five. She just pulled away.

Bad sport, I thought.

I went back to the bench and grabbed my towel and near-empty water bottle. Following everyone out of the gym, I entered the dressing room and the excitement.

"We rule!" a voice came from the back of the room.

I started a chant. "We're number one!"

Jessie jumped in, "We're number one!"

"Guys." Grace stood up on the bench so we could all see her. "We better not . . . their locker room is right next door."

Talk about a nice person — Grace wouldn't harm a fly, or its family. Last year in Mr. Philips' class, she took the blame for ketchup stains on the whiteboard simply because no one else would admit to it. We all knew Henri had done it. His mom gave him ketchup packages when she dropped off his fast-food lunch. I wished my mom would let me eat fast food sometimes. But that's not my point. The amazing thing was that, in Grace's mind, she had seen the ketchup being sprayed and had done nothing. As good as guilty. I think they call that an accomplice. The next day she guilted Henri into confessing and the case was closed.

"Grace's right," Emma said, untying her long thick ponytail. "They know we killed them out there. We don't need to rub it in their faces. The important thing is that we're number one!"

I started another chant. "We're number one! We're number one!" But it took me a second to clue in. "Oh, right. Sorry."

Jessie said, "I think the coach should say a few words."

I looked at her like she had lost her mind. "I don't want Coach in here."

"Not him." Jessie smiled. "You."

I stood up on the bench next to Grace. "First of all, I'm not the coach. It's *assistant* coach. Second, we owe the game to Jessie. Good one, Jessie!" After a round of applause, I waited for everyone to quiet down. "I also want to thank everyone for coming to the extra practices and helping to get us to first place in the league!"

I waited for a huge round of applause. But I found myself surprised when it got cut short by Caitlyn. She ran crying from the locker room.

Was it something I said?

"Well, what are you all waiting for?" Grace clapped her hands. "Let's go after her."

I was the last out of the locker room and back in the gym. The Warriors had long cleared out and it was just Coach Philip talking to Caitlyn. She was still crying. When the coach saw everyone thundering into the gym, he said, "Okay, girls, gather around."

I stood next to Jessie and she grabbed my hand. This didn't seem like good news.

Coach cleared his throat. "Well, there's really no easy way to put this."

A thousand things ran through my brain. *The last game didn't count and we're not in first place. The league ran out of money and it's shutting down. The gym ran out of money and is shutting down.* But why was Caitlyn crying?

Coach cleared his throat one more time. "Caitlyn's leaving the team."

Caitlyn's sobs got louder as a hush spread through the players. I asked the first question that popped into my brain. "Caitlyn, why?"

It took her a moment. "Well, I'm not leaving because I want to. I love you guys. It's just that . . . I'm moving. To Vancouver."

"What?! That means you're leaving this school and everything!"

Caitlyn nodded.

I turned to Coach. "Did you know?"

"Her mom told me about two weeks ago. Caitlyn and I were going to tell you then, but I think she was hoping her dad's new job would somehow not go through."

Caitlyn shook her head. It looked like she couldn't speak.

"Plus," Coach continued, "Caitlyn didn't want her last game as a Hornet to be a sad one. She wanted it to be a great one."

In front of the crowd a hand went up. "Now's maybe not the best time to ask," Natalie said, "but how does that affect me?"

Natalie played on the second line and subbed in for me when I got tired, which was pretty much never. She wanted to know if Caitlyn's spot was now hers.

Coach Philip waved his hands in front of his face. "You have to let me finish. We're all really sad to see Caitlyn go, but there's more news . . . more to the story."

The whole team erupted into questions. *What next? What secrets have people been keeping from each other? The moment we clinch first place, how could we start to lose valuable players? How could things be so unfair?*

"Now, hold on. Just —"

This time I interrupted the coach. "Who else is leaving?"

He shook his head. "It's not who's leaving, but rather who's joining. Give me one second."

He jogged through the gym doors, and all eyes went back and forth between Caitlyn and the doors.

The doors opened and Coach came in with two people — a girl carrying a Warrior jersey, and her mother. She was taller than I am, and had her hair pulled back into a ponytail. She was Number 9, the one who got yelled at for missing the three-point shot.

Coach held out his hands. "Okay, Kate, go ahead."

My jaw practically hit the hardwood when the Warrior player took Caitlyn's Hornets jersey and pulled it on over her T-shirt.

The coach smiled, "Hornets, please welcome Kate to your starting lineup!"

There was absolute silence, except for one squeaky fan spinning high up on the ceiling.

Kate got a nudge from her mom and spoke. "I bet you're wondering what's going on. Basically, my family just moved, and I have to change schools to Forrestwood. I guess I just want to say that I'm really looking forward to meeting everyone and playing on your team."

More awkward silence until Coach broke in. "Welcome to the school, Kate. This is your first week here, right?"

"Yes."

Finally, it was Emma who asked what we were all thinking. "We haven't seen you in the halls. Whose class are you in?"

"Ms. Delancey."

That's a grade-eight class, I thought. *Is that allowed?* Ours was a grade-seven team.

Kate continued, "But my birthday's in December and Coach was nice enough to cut me a break because there's no room on the grade-eight team." She retreated back to the protection of her mother. I examined her. She had reddish hair and was about as tall as Jessie, which put her taller than me.

Coach ended the introduction with, "Welcome to the Hornets, Kate. I know you'll be a valuable addition to the team."

But she's not an addition, I thought. *She's replacing Caitlyn.* The shock of losing Caitlyn started to sink in. Caitlyn and I had a playing history together. We communicated without words during games. We could predict each other's next moves, and that sort of teamwork can't be built overnight.

In tears, I hugged Caitlyn. So did everyone else on the team.

I saw Grace go up to Kate and introduce herself.

As much as I was going to miss Caitlyn, it wouldn't be fair to not give Kate a chance, even though she used to be a Warrior. I decided to introduce myself. Not as assistant coach, just as captain.

3 POST GAME

By the time I got home I was already starting to get curious about Kate. After dinner, I typed her name into an internet search. But it was impossible to find any information without a last name. I had typed *Kate* and *Carrville Warriors* and hit enter. The screen streamed down a whole lot of weird links so I gave up and entered a new search: *Richmond Hill Hornets*. I clicked on the team website Coach built with another teacher so we could post game schedules, wins and losses, and photos if we had any. I logged on, *Renna*, and typed in the password *hornets* and my jersey number *18*. I scrolled down to the bottom where there was an area to send messages to my teammates. There was no one online, so I just left a short post.

18 says ... Hornets 54 Warriors 52.
Richmond Hill Hornets take first place
in their division. Good job, everybody!
We're sad to see you go, Caitlyn!

I heard my mom walking up the stairs, so I quickly logged out and clicked off the computer monitor. I rushed back into my room to finish my homework. Mom wouldn't let me have a computer in my room. It had to be in the open because my parents were afraid of the Internet and what it could do to me. I wished they would get with the times.

I had a hard time focusing on my homework. All I could think about was my team. I looked up at the posters on my wall. The big one above my desk was of Michael Jordan flying through the air, doing a one-handed slam dunk for the Chicago Bulls. Every basketball fan needed a picture of him. Next to my bedroom window were posters of two other players: Sylvia Fowles, Number 34, and Candice Dupree, Number 4. They both played for the WNBA team the Chicago Sky. I saw them play once against the Atlanta Dream, and it was the best day of my life. Why couldn't I be eighteen and play pro ball in WNBA already? My only hope was that, by the time I was old enough, there would be a Toronto team in the pro league.

My mind raced back to the Hornets. We won a big game, but what would losing Caitlyn do to the team? What would getting Kate do to the team? She was a Warrior. It would take her a while to get to know everyone, figure out the plays, and get with our game. I didn't want to lose first spot because of the time she needed to catch up.

I needed to vent. No one had been online, and Mom and Dad were on homework watch, so no phone calls. I had only one option. It wasn't a pretty one, but what choice did I have?

I tiptoed out my door and into my sister's room. Every time I went in, my eyes took a while to adjust to the colour scheme. Pink. Not just any pink. Bright, bubble-gum pink. Yuk! Instead of posters on the wall, Anita had two shelves. One with ponies and princesses, and the other with pony and princess DVDs. But what could I do? She was only eight.

Anita looked up from her bed. "Shouldn't you be doing homework?"

I smiled. "What's that under your book?"

"What? Nothing."

I spotted a rainbow-coloured tail sticking out of her math workbook. I went to reach for it, faked left, then moved in on the right and grabbed it.

She sat up. "Don't!"

I let go of the tail and shushed her. I checked the door for movement downstairs and then sat on her bed. "I need to talk."

She looked at me. "What about? Boys?!"

"No, not boys. Okay, you know Caitlyn?"

Anita shook her head.

"She plays on my team. At least, did play on my team. She's moving, and we get a new player instead, and that's a disaster for our team, right?"

"You lost me."

"You can't add a new team member in the middle of the season. Especially one from a rival team."

"What does 'rival' mean?"

I smacked my hands down on her bed in frustration. Her fluffy pink pillows bounced up into the air.

"Everything okay up here?" a deep voice suddenly broke in.

I looked up to see my dad. "Sorry. We were just talking."

"Well, Renna, finish your homework and then meet me outside."

I left Anita's pink fortress and hunched over my science homework. I managed to get one more paragraph of my report done before hearing the distinct *clang* a basketball makes when it bounces off the rusted basketball rim on my driveway. Even up in my room, I could tell that my dad had missed his shot!

I closed my books, turned off my desk lamp, and tore downstairs and outside.

"Done your work?" my dad asked as I hit the driveway.

I nodded. "Pretty much."

My dad bounced a basketball with two hands. "You should have seen that one. Almost a three-pointer."

"I could hear it upstairs. Nothing but rim." I tried not to laugh.

"Think you can do better?" He bounce-passed the

ball to me. "I shot from right here." He marked the distance from the net with his foot.

I don't pretend to be the best three-point shooter; that's why I play point guard. "From here?"

"Yes."

I lined up for the shot — knees bent, elbows bent — and, with a gentle push, sent the ball arching toward the net. It dropped in.

My dad lifted his arms in the air. "How did you do that?"

"Come here and I'll show you." I pulled him closer and put the ball in his hands. "Don't take your eyes off the net, okay?"

He nodded. "That's it?"

"And send the ball high and up. No line-drive shooting."

He bounced the ball and looked anxious to shoot. "That's it?"

Stepping out of his way, I said, "Try it."

He released the ball. It missed the net and bounced off the garage door.

I picked it up and dribbled it back to him. "Nice try."

Dad laughed.

"Seriously. This time, try some backspin."

"Okay." He dribbled the ball a few times, then grabbed it and held it up, ready to shoot.

"Dad?"

"Not now, I'm about to make this one."

"Okay."

The ball missed again, but this time he at least hit the rim.

"Dad, why do you shoot hoops with me?"

"Because I know you like to."

I smiled. "You suck though, right?"

"I know. But I'm a very good accountant."

I grabbed the ball. "You can do this. Let's take it back a bit. Have I told you about BEEF before?"

"But we raised you vegetarian."

"Not that kind of beef. Take the ball. BEEF: B, Balance on both feet. E, Elbows pointed to the net. That looks good."

He looked like he was very uncomfortable. "Now what?"

"The other E is for Extend your arms when you shoot; and F is for Follow through."

He stood at the net and said, "B,E,E,F. BEEF."

"Go for it."

He took his shot. I kept my eyes on my dad instead of on the ball. If his form was good, the ball stood a good chance of going in. I didn't hear the *clang*. Instead, I saw a big smile. He jumped up and down like his shot was a game winner.

"That was amazing! Where'd you get BEEF from?"

"My basketball coach from two seasons ago. He was amazing." When I said *basketball coach* I sighed. Not only did Mr. Philip not know what he was doing, but now the team had the new girl, who was the big un-known. Not the best combination for holding onto the number-one spot.

"Everything okay?"

I pushed the thoughts away and smiled. "Let's see you get two in a row."

4 THE STING

Five minutes to go before lunch and the science teacher gave everyone time to clean up. I think it was Mrs. Sherbet who needed the five minutes to sit at her desk and rest. People got recess detentions for calling Mrs. Herbert the name of a frosty treat. But there was no rule against thinking it.

Grace and Emma descended on the table that I shared with Jessie and two boys, and talk turned right away to the thing that had been bugging me. "So why do you think Kate switched teams? I mean, why would a Warrior want to be a Hornet?"

"She moved," Grace answered.

"Do you buy that, Grace?" I asked.

"I'll tell you what I think," Jessie said. "I think the Warriors kicked her off the team."

Grace looked puzzled. "Why would you say that?"

"Think about it. Maybe she wasn't any good." Jessie smiled, proud of her theory.

"You're right. She did miss that last big shot," I cut

in. "Emma, didn't you cover her?"

"Yeah, I covered her," said Emma.

"And?"

"Let me think. I didn't notice anything really good or bad about her game. She was tall and fast, but she didn't get the ball much. Her point guard was kind of ignoring her."

"Anything else?" I asked.

"Okay, okay," Emma said. "You're right, something did occur to me. Maybe she didn't switch teams because she moved."

Now she had my attention. "Then why?"

"What if the Warriors sent her to us?"

I rolled my eyes. Emma was the seventh-grade's great debater. She could talk teachers out of detentions, extra homework . . . anything. I gave her the benefit of the doubt and listened to her crazy theory.

"We're the number-one team, right?"

I nodded.

"So what if the Warriors found out that Caitlyn had to move teams? Maybe they had Kate become a Hornet so she could sink us. Get fouls, miss shots —"

We all broke out into laughter.

"There's no need to make so much noise," Mrs. Sherbet barked from the front of the class.

I stopped laughing and noticed that the two boys at my table were listening in on our conversation. I gave them a dirty look, and they looked away. Turning back to the girls, I asked, "Don't you hate this? We've put so much work into the team, and now this kind of puts us back."

"I even gave up a day at Wonderland with my family because of an extra Saturday morning practice," Jessie said.

"I remember that," I said. "We've worked so hard to get to number one and now Caitlyn's gone. Everything's up in the air."

Jessie shrugged her shoulders, "We'll find out how good Kate is at practice."

Emma hadn't given up yet. "Do we know anybody who knows her —"

Grace cut her off. "Shouldn't we relax and hope for the best?"

I smiled. "That's such a Grace line."

"I should hope so. I'm Grace."

As team captain, I didn't have the luxury of just waiting and hoping. I needed to know what was happening on and off the court. Forrestwood School has never won a championship, and I wanted our grade-seven team to be the first.

When the lunch bell rang, Mrs. Sherbet was first out the door. By the time I got to the hall, there were streams of bodies going in every direction. It was impossible not to bang into people or get banged into. When I made it in one piece to the top of the stairwell, I started to turn toward the hall where the grade-seven lockers were.

But then I spotted Kate. She was pulling a lunch bag out of an expensive all-pink Roots backpack. I knew it was expensive because I had wanted the same one, but I couldn't get my mom or dad to buy it for me.

I took a deep breath and walked over to her. It took a few seconds for Kate to look up. It was kind of like when we call my cousins overseas in Chandigarh, there's always a delay. When Kate and I finally made eye contact, I put on my best smile.

"Hi!"

Kate did not return the smile. She just nodded.

"So, I'm glad I found you, because I wanted to officially welcome you to the team. I'm the captain, Renna Rashad."

I held out my hand for a handshake. Kate just stared at me like I had something dangling from my nose. I moved my hand up for a high-five, thinking, *Maybe the shake's too formal for her.* Wrong.

I tried again. "Look, I know how hard it is to move and adjust to a new school. When I was in grade one, my parents decided to move out of Toronto and it was so hard. But, like anything, I got used to it. And I guess that's my point. You will too."

Kate's dark brown eyes were no longer pointed at my face. Instead, it looked like she was staring at something sitting on my left shoulder.

"What position do you like to play? Centre? Guard?" She was a brick wall. Well, I had done my best as team captain to welcome her aboard. I decided to close with, "If you wanna talk basketball sometime, come bug me. And a reminder — we have a practice tomorrow after school."

Kate turned, put her backpack into her locker, and slammed it shut, extra hard.

I was confused. Was she angry? Had I said something wrong?

"Renna, right?"

She spoke! It was a miracle! I wanted to run around her in a celebration dance, but decided to hold off. "Yep. Renna. Team capt—"

"Lose that stupid smile and get lost."

Huh? I stood, frozen, waiting for Kate to add, *ha-ha, just kidding* or something. Instead, she brushed past me, her shoulder digging into me hard enough to force me into a locker. I hit it and bounced back in a lot of pain and confusion. She'd done that on purpose. *What a beast!*

5 HEAD TO HEAD

The next morning, I wanted to tell Jessie about angry Kate. But the crowded school hallway was not the best place to break the news. So I swallowed my anger and played along like everything was okay.

"You okay, Renna?"

I looked at Jessie. *Am I that bad an actor?* I mumbled back, "I'm fine."

"Well, if you want to talk, I'm here."

"I just didn't sleep well." At least that was the truth.

We arrived at the blue change-room door and entered.

"There they are," Emma said.

Everyone looked up, including Kate, who was tying her shoelaces. The last time I saw her she was shoving me into a locker. I tried not to look at her, but I couldn't help noticing that she looked weird in my team's uniform.

"You know you don't have to wear your uniform to practice," Jessie said to Kate.

"I know. I guess I'm just excited to wear it."

Kate smiled innocently, but I didn't buy it. I chose to sit as far away from her as possible in the small room. I took my time and, by the time I entered the court, everyone was already doing laps.

"Hey, assistant, I was waiting for you." Coach smiled at me. "You're usually first out here." He pulled me to centre court, out of the way of the runners. "I wanted to run this play by you. It's called a Full Court No Bounce Play."

He flipped through a pile of papers on his clipboard, until he found the page he wanted. He held it up to me, and I smiled when I saw the *www* address printed on the bottom. I looked at the picture and started to read the details, but I had to stop because I was starting to feel dizzy. Around me, everyone was running. I spotted Kate, who was circling like a shark. I felt even worse when I saw her talking with Jessie.

"It seems okay." I hastily handed the paper back to the coach and joined the runners.

I circled a few times before I caught up with Jessie. "Everything okay?"

"Yeah, why?"

"No reason." *Focus on the practice*, I told myself. The Hornets were *my* team. Kate could push me around a thousand times but that wouldn't change.

"Phweew!" The coach blew his whistle and shouted, "Suicides!"

I have a love/hate relationship with suicides. They burn, but they make me a stronger sprinter. I met up with everyone at the baseline.

Coach blew his whistle again and I took off, first to the free-throw line and back, and then to the black line on top of the key. My muscles were aching. I looked sideways to see where I was in the pack. Grace and Jessie were in stride with me, because one was short and fast and the other had long legs. I took in short, loud breaths on my way back to the baseline. I touched it with my fingertips and turned toward half court. I pushed myself at ninety percent, saving just a little extra for the longest stretch to come.

Hating the coach for making me do this, I touched the half-court line and headed back.

There and back to go.

This was the point in the suicides which separated the runners into the good, bad, and ugly. I touched the black baseline, glanced over, and saw Kate.

I can't let her win.

I whipped around and pushed with everything my legs would give me. The walls of the gym blurred as I sped by the half-court line and touched the far baseline.

Last stretch for home.

My arms and legs worked like a machine and I stuck my head out as the finish line came into sight. I crossed the black line just ahead of Kate, and quickly realized that I had a bigger problem. There was no room to stop. I smashed into the blue padding on the walls and bounced back, still on my feet. Next to me, Kate was on the floor, out of breath. I smiled to myself. That felt good.

"Wow," Coach said. "I don't think I've seen two people run so hard. Shake it off and go get a drink."

I hobbled over to the water fountain with Jessie and Natalie.

"You're drenched." Natalie said.

"And you could've injured yourself," Jessie added.

I crouched over the water fountain and drank for what seemed like a full minute. I stood up and wiped cold water from my face. "But I won."

"Didn't know it was a race. Kind of looked like you were showing off in front of the new girl," Jessie said.

I shook my head. "Are you just mad that you lost?" I entered the basketball court ready for more.

Coach Philip held up his hand. "Form a circle around me." Holding up one of his Internet printouts, he waited until everyone was quiet. "I wanted to try this, but it's just too confusing. So, we're going to do two-on-ones again.

"Again?" Emma whined.

"Well, it's not new to you, but it is to Kate. And there's nothing wrong with making sure our basics are strong. Right, Renna?" Coach answered, looking at me.

I nodded as seriously as I could. Coach doesn't have a lot of plays in his repertoire. And as hard as he tries, he never comes across as what a coach should be — a leader. Instead, he's more like our supervisor.

Kate raised her hand. "Coach?"

"Yes, Kate?"

"Are we doing regular two-on-ones?"

"I guess I should have explained. You see, you line up . . . in groups of three . . . and then, well —"

I jumped in, "We're keeping the same threes." But I wasn't thinking. With Caitlyn gone, that meant . . .

"Okay, we're keeping the same threes. The only change is to Renna's line, because Kate's replacing Caitlyn." He blew his whistle and shouted in what he must have thought was a motivating way, "Let's go, go, go!"

Everyone took off, grabbing basketballs and standing behind the net, except me.

"Everything okay, Renna?" Coach asked.

I sucked in my pride, nodded my head, and joined the group. Natalie was waiting for me with Kate, who was dribbling a basketball. I reached into the big metal basketball container and pulled one out.

"Renna, you going to debrief Kate?"

I looked at Kate, but spoke to Natalie. I had no need to communicate with someone who didn't want to communicate with me. "We're going to use this basketball, and you can go ahead and tell her."

"Well . . ." Natalie stalled, collected her thoughts. "It's basically two-on-one. We take turns playing defence. Kate, you're in the middle, so you try to stop Renna and me from scoring. Next time, when you get back in line, one of us will be in the middle on defence. When you see it, it will make sense. Did I get that right, Renna?"

I nodded.

"Full court?" Kate asked.

I stopped dribbling. "That a problem?"

"Bring it on," Kate responded.

On the baseline, we waited in our three lines for our turn at the net. Natalie took the far left, I took the right side, and Kate was stuck in the middle on defence.

Ahead of us, Jessie, Grace, and Emma started their two-on-one. On defence, Grace dribbled the ball just ahead of her two partners. She passed the ball to Jessie, who started to drive it forward. Jessie whipped it to Emma as Grace tried to cover the pass. The girls passed back and forth a few times until they approached the net. Emma faked a layup and passed the ball behind her back to Jessie, who drove to the net. Jessie did an easy layup, her height taking her above Grace's reach.

Coach clapped his hands. He shot me a look, so I joined in, clapping my hands. I shouted across court to Grace, telling her that next time she should keep her hands up high and drive Jessie to the wall.

It was our turn. Kate took the defensive position and picked up the ball.

"Whenever you're ready, pass it to them," Coach said.

While Kate was distracted by Coach's instructions, I turned to Natalie on my far left. I pointed to myself and made the international sign for basketball shot. Since Natalie was my sub, she usually did whatever I told her to.

Kate passed the ball to Natalie. *Whatever*, I thought. Natalie dribbled it up court and passed it ahead to me. Keeping Kate on the move, I dribbled fast up to the half-court line and whipped it to Natalie, who barely caught it. Kate moved to cover Natalie, and I waved my arms in the air, ready for the pass. Natalie tried a lob pass, up and over Kate, but Kate managed to deflect it a little. I recovered, grabbed the ball, and went in for my signature layup. The ball spun around the rim. To my shock, it didn't flop in.

Kate circled around, showing her proud face, and grabbed the ball to send back to the next defender.

Walking back, I said to Natalie, "That was a bad pass."

"I'm sorry."

"Focus more. Next time we have to get it in."

I barely paid attention as the next groups took their turns. I was concentrating hard on beating Kate. When it was time for us to go again, I stood facing Natalie and Kate, bouncing the ball. Then I bounce-passed to Natalie and started to move back, balancing on my toes so I could pivot, with my hands up so I could block a pass, high or low. I applied pressure to Natalie so she would pass to Kate, and when she did I almost got some skin on the ball. I moved back quickly while Kate brought the ball to half court. My defensive pressure on Kate pushed her deeper toward the net and I cut off her angle, keeping her from a layup or passing to Natalie. Kate faked around me, and then turned to release the ball to a wide-open Natalie.

I can't believe the Beast fell for it, I thought.

That's when I swatted the ball down and out of bounds. I smiled wide and cried, "Denied!" I walked back, letting Kate and Natalie fetch the ball.

"Feeling better?" Jessie asked.

"Renna is back," I declared.

"You should go easier on the new girl."

"Uh-huh." I held back a laugh and thought about how it was the new girl who was the problem, not me.

Emma looked back. "Nice one, Renna."

"Thank you. It's really nice to feel some appreciation around here."

Rounding back to the group, Natalie jumped in. "You know what, Renna?"

"What?"

"You're awesome."

"Why, thank you, Natalie. You know what?"

"What?" She smiled waiting for the returned compliment.

"You're up!" I laughed, faking a chest-pass to her and laughing.

"Oh!"

We turned back to the practice to see the ball roll

down the court to Jessie's line. Jessie wasted no time, driving it hard to the net and scoring. Then it was our turn again. *How's this going to work?* I asked myself. Natalie was ready to go on defence and Kate on my other side. *Do I have to pass to the Beast?*

Natalie dribbled the ball. "Ready?"

I nodded, received her pass, and brought it out. Natalie played it smart and covered Kate tightly, so it was almost impossible to pass to her. I dribbled the ball over the half-court line and slowed down. I stared at the open line to the net, and the net stared back at me. Problem was, I could hear Jessie's voice telling me, "You should go easier on the new girl." So I passed the ball in the direction of both Natalie and Kate. Hard. Natalie reached for it, but she couldn't hold onto it. Kate grabbed it and took it down the left line. I yelled out, "I'm open," because Natalie was still scrambling to get back into the play. Instead, Kate ignored me, drove it to the net, and made the layup.

Kate let out a whoop, "Whoo-hoo!"

I turned around and made my way toward the gym doors. I shouted out, "Drink," before the coach could ask where I was going. Out in the hallway, I paced back and forth at the fountain with one thought bouncing around in my head. *How am I going to play with her?* After forgetting to take a drink I walked back and pulled on the gym door. On the other side was Kate.

She pushed through the door and waited for it to

close. "You're not as good as they say you are."

What? I looked over her shoulder at the two small windows in the gym door. The team was busy practising. I wished they had an idea of what was happening on this side of the door.

"So stay out of my way. On and off the court."

As Kate moved past me back into the gym, she clipped my foot, hard, with her shoe.

It sent me off balance and I had to reach out to the wall for support. I leaned back, out of sight from everyone in the gym, and tried hard to hold back a tear. Why me? What did I do to Kate?

6 READ BETWEEN THE LINES

"So let me get this straight," Jessie said pulling a red apple from her lunch bag. "This is Kate you're talking about?"

"Yes."

"And she's doing what to you?"

I lowered my voice to bring zero attention to me in the hallway. "She's been bugging me."

"So tell her to stop."

"I don't think that's possible." I wanted to tell Jessie the whole story, but I was holding back. I didn't want to sound like a wimp and a victim. I'm a doer, not a complainer. Always have been, always would be.

Jessie crunched into her apple and started toward the lunchroom. "She's new. She has to be feeling like an outsider." She chewed on a big piece of apple. "Maybe you just have to give her some room. And as long as we keep winning, you probably don't care what she does off the court. Know what I mean?"

"I guess." I looked down at the teeth marks in her

apple. She had a good point. "I'm just confused."

Jessie stopped at the entrance to the lunchroom. "As captain — and you're an incredible captain — you're used to everyone loving you, trusting you. Maybe you need to back off a little in that department."

"Back off? Me? You know me better than anyone else. When it comes to sports there's only two settings — on and off."

Behind me, a lunchroom monitor with a red and yellow construction vest interrupted. "Move it, ladies. No idling in the hallway."

I rolled my eyes at her and followed Jessie to the Hornets' table. Jessie sat down beside Grace and started trading lunches. Natalie was busy with the other two subs, Monica and Camilla. The three of them were hunched over Camilla's iPod touch, covering it up like it was illegal. And it was! Everything cool was banned by the school. If Jessie didn't get what was going on, I wondered if anyone else would. I decided to start with Emma, who had just sat down next to me. "How's it going?"

"Okay." She dug a plastic fork into a piece of chicken. "You?"

"Okay, I guess."

"Good practice last night." When she lifted the fork, it sagged with the weight of the chicken.

"Think so?"

Emma chewed and covered up her mouth with her

palm before talking. "Why do you say that?"

I threw a softball. "I miss Caitlyn."

"We all do."

"And Kate. She kind of rubs me the wrong way."

"Really? She played better than I expected."

"So you thought maybe she'd suck?"

"I'm not saying that. You are." Emma jabbed the fork into another piece of chicken. I was surprised it didn't break. "What are you getting at?"

"We're playing a really good team tomorrow and I'm just worried about it. Everyone's worked so hard to get to number one and I'm not so sure we can hold on to it."

"Because of Kate?"

I backed off. "I don't know." Watching Emma eat made me hungry, so I unwrapped my sandwich and took a bite.

"I understand why you're worried. A new person can really shake the team's dynamics."

"That's exactly what I'm saying." Now to get Emma on my side and get Kate off the team. "Don't you want to win? Hold that trophy up in the air?

"Renna, you have nothing to worry about. She's a strong forward. I can see it."

"Uh-huh."

"I know you're just doing your job as captain, but don't worry so much."

Just like that, the bubble I had sent up was popped.

When I turned back to the rest of the group, everyone was gathered around the fancy MP3 player. Jessie and Monica each had an earphone in, and they were bouncing to the music. Natalie got up to recycle what she could of her lunch, and I got an idea. "Hey, Natalie."

"Yeah?"

Time to toss a hardball. "You must really be upset with Kate."

"Why would you say that?" She examined a plastic juice bottle.

"Oh, I don't know —"

She interrupted me. "Where does this go?"

"Plastic goes in blue."

"But it has a paper label on it."

"True."

She peeled off the label and tossed it into the white bin. The bottle went into the blue bin. "You were saying?"

"If I was you, I'd think it sucked that a new girl from another team gets a spot on the front line."

When she didn't answer, I pushed harder. "You've been working hard as a substitute player and would make a good starter, but Kate walks in and takes your spot."

I watched Natalie think about what I said. I egged her on. "You could always complain."

"You know what, though? She has a lot more experience than I do. Anyhow, it's the coach's decision."

For the first time ever, I began to wish that my teammates weren't so nice.

"Well, if you're happy with second —"

"Hey, everyone!"

I turned in midsentence to see Kate walking up to our table. She was flanked by two grade-eight girls.

"Hey, Kate," Natalie said, "We were just talking about you."

Kate eyed me. "You were?"

"Hi, Kate." Grace looked up from the iPod touch. Jessie and Monica took out their earpieces.

Kate held up her lunch bag. "Mind if me and my friends join you?"

I looked around the table. Everyone was bright-eyed and smiling. They were excited to get to hang out with grade eights. Grade eights were a world above us.

"Sure," Jessie said.

Kate and her friends sat down.

I didn't pay attention.

"Excited for your first game, Kate?" Grace asked.

"Totally. I hope you guys think I did a good job. I was so nervous at practice."

Emma said, "You did great."

I lost my appetite.

"It's just tough being the new one, and I wasn't sure what everyone thought of me."

Oh, she's playing it up big time! I thought.

Emma told Kate that she had a really good practice, but that it was up to me, the team captain, to decide.

Kate ignored the part about me. "Oh, that's so good

to hear, Emma. I was really worried." She turned to Camilla, "Is that an iPhone?"

"No, it's an iPod touch. It's an old one, so there's no speakers."

"That's still cool. Check this out. I just got it." Kate reached into her pocket and pulled out a shiny black gadget.

"An iPhone?" Emma practically had her tongue sticking out of her mouth.

"Yep."

Everyone around the table seemed to melt. Jealousy filled the air like a bad odour. That's another difference between grade seven and grade eight. Grade sevens get toys and grade eights get phones.

Kate tossed it to Emma like it wasn't an extremely expensive thing of beauty. "Just don't make any long-distance calls."

Emma laughed as she was immediately swarmed by the other girls. A few buttons were pushed and a song poured out of the phone, getting the girls even more excited.

I watched from a distance, pretending not to care. Getting Kate off the team had just become impossible. I could shout from the school rooftop that she was a violent beast and nobody would believe me. How could my situation get any worse?

That question was answered when two grade-eight boys stopped by the table to say hi to Kate and her friends. Another big difference between grade seven and grade eight. Boys.

7 DON'T BRING ME DOWN

Six minutes into the third quarter in our game against the Bulls. I had hoped Kate would be friendly to me for the sake of the team. I couldn't have been more wrong. She forced me to play as though the entire left side of the court didn't exist.

The Bulls brought the ball across half court and into Hornet territory, enjoying home-court advantage. It was always hard to play in another school's gym. I found my player to cover, the point guard for the Bulls. She had a pretty good passing arm. With my arms up and my hands stretched out, I forced her to pass low down and grabbed the ball when she did. The Bulls retreated into position and I slowly dribbled the ball forward, allowing my team to find their spots. The scoreboard read 34–28 for the Bulls. Our first-place spot was officially endangered.

I shouted out, "Find an opening!" and scanned the horizon. Wanting to make a pass play and score a quick bucket, I shouted out again, "Hustle! Hustle!" I couldn't go left because of Kate, so when Grace stepped in front of my cover, I rolled right.

"Open!"

I looked up and spotted Emma deep on the right side, cutting forward and backward. When she cut forward again, I tossed the ball up high and over her. She quickly cut back and caught the ball, planted her feet, shot, and scored.

"Thanks, Renna," she called.

"Nice one." I high-fived her as I rolled back to half court.

Unfortunately, the point didn't help because the Bulls stormed in and scored right away. I stared at the scoreboard, hoping it would magically change and put us in the lead. This game was proving to be not much fun, just hard work and stress.

Grace clapped her hands together. "Let's make it happen!"

She seemed so optimistic that I passed the ball to her. She brought it up on the left side. I tried to lose my cover by rolling right and doing a figure-eight around Emma. Standing with a perfect line to the net, I yelled out to Grace, "Grace, pass!"

"Huh?" That's when I noticed that Grace didn't have the ball. Kate did. Mean beast or not, she was on the team. I was open and had a chance to bring us back into this game. So I raised my hands high.

Kate ignored my raised hands. She drove the ball to

the net and was swatted away by a Bulls left forward.

I let out a, "Come on!" even though it wouldn't make any difference to Kate. I shot Coach a look of frustration, but he seemed as out-to-lunch as usual.

Positioned under our net, Jessie stopped the Bulls from scoring. The Hornets' boat was sinking, but at least there weren't any new holes.

From behind the baseline, Jessie passed me the ball and I brought it up. Cranking my neck to the left I checked the scoreboard. We were still down by six, and the seconds were eating away at the third quarter. I had to play it extra cautious, because I didn't have Caitlyn to pass the ball to. Kate had not passed to me once during the game, and there was no way I was going to feed her the ball.

The rest of my teammates were sweaty and tired. Jessie was overwhelmed with elbows. Emma, on the right side, couldn't get open, and Grace, on my left side, was struggling against a taller player. I had to make a move, so I one-armed the ball to Jessie under the net. The Bull centre grabbed it and threw it to the person who should have been covering Kate. I guess she had figured out that I wouldn't pass to that corner. The Bulls right forward took the breakaway and scored two points. A moment later the buzzer rang. I walked to the bench with my head hung low.

"Okay, everyone," Coach Philip said. "Get some water and rest up. It's only eight points and we can still do it."

I had my head draped in a towel and my hands over my eyes. The darkness felt good. No one was worried that a new girl would mess up the team's dynamics. The break ended and I dragged myself back onto the court. Behind me, Natalie, Monica, and Camilla cheered, hoping that they'd get called off the bench to play.

The referee looked at me and the Bulls centre and asked, "Ready?"

I nodded.

He threw the ball in the air and I swatted at it, sending it back to Grace. Ten minutes and eight points stood between a win and a loss, a loss that would mean a downgrade to second place.

I moved far right and let Grace bring the ball forward.

For a small girl, she had a loud voice. "Let's go, Hornets! Scramble!"

Scramble was code for, well, scrambling around and shaking off the defence. I moved to the far right side and watched Grace pass the ball to Kate. Moving up the right side, I looked for a line on the net, even though I was never going to get the ball. Kate stopped dribbling in three-point range and I knew she'd go for it. *There's more than one way to get the ball from her,* I thought. When she released it, I sprinted toward the net for the rebound. I wanted Kate's ball more than anything. The ball bounced off the rim and I jumped up in the crowd to get it. The ball landed in my hands and I was about to lay it up when I heard a whistle. "What?"

The referee pointed at me. "Number 18 Hornets, foul. Two shots for the Bulls, Number 24."

"Foul?" Could he mean me?

"Elbowing."

I was fuming mad.

Grace walked back with me. "It's okay, Renna. It happens."

"I guess." I gathered around the key, opposite the Bulls point guard, and watched and prayed as Bulls Number 24 lined up for two shots.

Please miss. Please, please.

"Face the net, elbows out!" the Bulls coach yelled. He sounded like he knew what he was doing. The ball soared into the air. Closing my eyes might have been silly, but I couldn't look.

"Nice try."

I was happy to hear the Bulls coach's words. It meant Number 24 had missed. She took her second shot, and I opened my eyes just enough to see the outline of the ball land right in the net.

Coach Philip called out, "Time, please."

The ref responded with, "Two-minute timeout called by the Hornets."

Natalie passed me my water and I guzzled it while Coach paced back and forth.

"I guess they're a good team. I'm just confused why we're not making points. I know I'm not an expert, but let's just get back out there and do our best.

Anything to add, Renna?"

Usually I have something to say to help the team, but this time I just shook my head. Without a left side, how could we win?

"Anyone else want to say anything?"

Jessie raised her hand. "I'm getting double-teamed under the net. So getting rebounds isn't happening."

Why was I continuing to let Kate bring me down? I had to remind myself that *I* was team captain. The timeout ended and it was our ball.

I approached Grace on my way to the baseline.

"What's up?" Grace asked.

"I need you to bring the ball up and then pass it to me."

"Sure, what did you have in mind?"

"I'm going to be on the right side and then cut in. I need a good pass."

Grace nodded her head. "Okay. What if you're not open?"

"I'll be open."

I took Grace's position as shooting guard and waited for her to dribble the ball into Bulls territory. Once she crossed over, I cut in between Grace and her cover, and lost my cover in the process. I hustled to the right side, then used my knees to cut sharply left, and landed in the exact spot where I wanted Grace to pass the ball. She did, and I grabbed it.

Instead of moving forward, like everyone would

expect, I stepped back into three-point territory and lined up for the shot. *BEEF.* Balanced on two feet, I stuck my elbows out and extended my arms, following them right through until my fingers pointed to the net. I watched the ball sail through the air and swoosh into the net. Three points! Only six to go. It felt great to take charge and act like a captain. I took high-fives from everyone — well, everyone except for Kate.

"How'd you know?" Grace asked.

"I didn't know, but we're doing it again."

When the Bulls returned, Jessie blocked our net and didn't let anyone or anything through. I turned to Grace. "Same thing, but I'm going deeper."

Grace smiled. "Happy to sub-in as point guard."

My defender seemed stressed as I readied myself to pounce. Grace crossed the half-court line and I took off. Jetting toward the net, I pivoted hard to the right and almost collided with Emma. My cover held up her hands to show she wasn't fouling anyone, and took the opportunity to go deep.

"Incoming!" Grace yelled.

I looked crosscourt to Kate and smiled. The ball landed over my head, but in my hands. Moving my right foot one step back, I confirmed that I was in three-point range and raised the ball. *BEEF* was all I thought launching the ball into the air. I almost couldn't believe it when the gym fell silent and everyone heard the unmistakable *swoosh* that only a three-pointer can make.

"Oh, my!" Coach Philip jumped up and down on the sidelines.

Grace approached me with eyes wide open. "You did it!"

"*We* did it." I turned to the ref and shouted out, "Timeout!"

The ref looked at me. "A player can't call it."

"Coach," I yelled. "Call a timeout."

"Timeout!"

I waved the team toward me, under our net. Kate came too, but I didn't care. I looked up at the coach for his approval, and he waved back at me with a small smile.

"What are we doing?" Emma asked.

"Clock's at thirty-five seconds and we're three behind," I said.

Jessie stepped forward. "You going for another three-pointer?"

I looked at her. "What choice do we have? Two points and we lose. Three points and we at least tie and keep the number-one spot."

"Good point, but the Bulls are kind of going to expect it," Jessie warned.

"That's why I'm going to bring it up this time. Then I'm going to feed it sideways to Grace and we're running the same play as last time."

"You going short or deep?" Grace asked.

"Expect both."

Grace nodded.

I clapped my hands. "Let's do this, Hornets." I dribbled, but my excitement transferred to the ball and it barely stayed in my hand. At the half-court line, I was surprised to see the Bulls take the double-team off Jessie and put it on me.

I faked right and then left before passing it sideways to Grace. The instant the ball was out of my hands, I shot forward, dividing my double-team in two. They retreated, but I kept them off my tail by zigzagging. The craziness threw the entire Bulls defence out of whack. I held my right hand up, signalling Grace to pass me the ball.

Grace yelled out, "Scramble!" Brilliant move, because it confused the Bulls even more.

Grace whipped the ball at me. It took two hands for me to get a handle on it. I looked up and repeated the word *BEEF* to myself. The game clock was running down — it was an all-or-nothing shot. The ball felt heavy in my hand as I released it. I jumped up, ready to celebrate a tie like I've never celebrated before.

The ball hit the rim.

Then, out of a sea of heads bobbing up and down for a rebound, Kate's popped up. She grabbed the ball and stuffed it in the net as the buzzer groaned. *We lose by one stupid point,* I thought. But then a voice cut through my disappointment.

"Foul, Bulls Number 9. Hornets get two shots."

I looked up in shock. We'd been brought back from the dead. Kate pranced around the court, collecting high-fives like they were hundred-dollar bills. When she passed me she held up her hand. I hesitantly lifted mine and smiled. Did this mean things were okay now? I reached for her hand and she pulled away, smiling evilly at me. I shook my head.

The team continued to celebrate until the coach cooled everyone down.

From the key everyone watched the intensity on Kate's face as she prepared to shoot. *Swoosh*. Her first shot was nothing but net. The game was tied.

She quickly reloaded and, again, *swoosh*. Just like that, we'd stolen the game from the Bulls.

Everyone piled on Kate in celebration except for me. Not only did she steal the win from under me, but that game-winning, all-star moment made her an official Hornet. I'd never felt so detached from my team.

8 NEW REALITY

Maybe it was the glowing red light from my alarm clock that kept me awake. I'd like to think that, but I knew the truth. I'd been tossing and turning for hours as I replayed what had been going on between Kate and me in my head. Finally, I knew what I had to do.

I got up and went down the hall to the office and typed *I have a bully* into an Internet search. I got 23,800,000 results. I never thought a number that wasn't a game score could bring comfort to me, but it did. That meant there were other people — lots of other people — dealing with the same problem. They were nameless and faceless, and probably from all around the world, but I felt connected. If there was only a way to find someone, maybe in Australia, and reach out to them. We could share our stories and help each other. I changed my search to *how to stop a bully*. There were a lot fewer hits, but eleven million was still a lot! I skimmed the first five sites, but they weren't saying anything Mrs. Sherbet hadn't told us.

Fed up, I reached to turn off the monitor and remembered that I hadn't logged onto the team website to see what everyone was posting after the win. I had one flashing message.

23 says... Hello? anyone?

Twenty three? That was Caitlyn's jersey number!

18 says... Caitlyn?

23 says... Renna!

18 says... How are you? I miss you!

23 says... Me too.

18 says... What time is it in Vancouver?

23 says... Just after eight. I miss Richmond Hill. How's the team?

18 says... Okay.

23 says... Okay? That's all you have to say?

18 says... Things aren't the same without you.

23 says... What do you mean?

18 says... The girl who replaced you is really bringing down the team.

23 says... Really? That's not what Grace said.

18 says... You spoke with Grace already?

23 says... She is my best friend.

18 says... True.

23 says... Are you okay?

I had two choices. I could reach out to Caitlyn and tell her everything, but risk it getting back to Grace and the rest of the team. Or I could shut up and pretend like everything was good.

23 says… You still there?

18 says… Caitlyn, I've tried to reach out, but nobody understands what I'm going through. I'm just feeling scared.

23 says… You're never scared. What is it?

18 says… Everything.

23 says… I'm confused.

18 says… Me too.

23 says… My mom's telling me to get off. Talk soon. Bye.

18 says… Bye.

I logged off the team website, and tiptoed to the washroom. I ran the water, and took a sip from the tap like it was a water fountain. When I stood back up, I looked at myself in the mirror and wondered about something that I hadn't ever had to think about. Was Kate bullying me because my skin is brown? Was it because of my name? Was it because my family comes from India? But did it matter why she was bullying me, when I couldn't bring myself to tell anyone that it was actually happening?

I flicked off the lights and made my way back to my

room in the dark. I flopped down on my bed with the realization that Kate had me cornered. From Richmond Hill to Vancouver and back, there was no escaping the fact that I couldn't shake Kate off my back. Renna vs. Kate. I'd had home-court advantage and had lost.

I flipped over my pillow so the cool side was up and watched the red glow of my alarm clock turn to midnight. It was hard to sleep feeling this lonely. With basketball in my life, I'd never felt alone. I had always felt like my teammates were more than friends, more like sisters. Too bad I had never told them how I felt. All they saw when they looked at me was a girl who hates losing. Whether or not I wanted to admit it, they were right. *So what does that make me now?*

I didn't want to fall asleep anymore, not if it would mean waking up and having to deal with the reality that I was fading away.

9 DIVIDED AND CONQUERED

I twirled my locker combo with my thumb. When the metal door popped open, I pulled out my lunch.

"Hi!"

It was Jessie. Maybe it was that she was in a good mood, or maybe it was that my best friend didn't know how miserable I was. But for some reason I felt a switch go off inside me and I started to cry. I've never felt so much water come out of my eyes. I lowered my head to hide it.

Jessie stared at me, not blinking. "Renna, you okay?"

I felt her hand on my shoulder. Between shivering bursts of tears, I mumbled, "I don't cry."

Jessie laughed.

The tears slowly stopped.

"What's wrong?"

"I thought you're supposed to feel better after you cry. I don't feel better."

"Renna, this is a hard and stressful time. I see what you're going through."

My water-logged vision made Jessie blurry as I looked up at her. "You do?"

"Yeah. This team is your team. You've put so much into it. We may not say it, but everyone really appreciates it. Then everything changes, and what are you supposed to do?"

What? I pulled away from her. "You're talking about the team. I'm upset about —"

"Renna, I know you miss Caitlyn, but I really think Kate has brought new energy to our line."

"I'm not talking about missing Caitlyn!"

"What about Caitlyn?" came a voice from behind us.

Other than Kate, I turned to find the one person I didn't want to talk to about what was happening. "Nothing," I mumbled.

Grace smiled. "Good, then let's go for lunch."

I knew Grace well enough to know that she would refuse to believe that Kate was capable of bullying.

In the lunchroom, the Hornets had gathered around our table. I could hear the unmistakable voice of Kate; loud and obnoxious. She turned and smiled as we approached.

"Hey, Jess."

I rolled my eyes as far as they would go.

"I was just inviting everyone to my house after school," Kate continued.

"After school? That sounds great!" Jessie said.

Kate's glance skipped over me as she invited Jessie

to sit. As Jessie moved to a seat, she grabbed my hand and forced me down beside her.

I had to get away. "Jessie, I've got to go to my lock —"

Kate cut me off and picked up where she left off. "So, my parents are working late and I thought we could take over the family room and watch the big-screen TV."

Jessie nodded. "Sounds like fun."

It was obvious that Grace, Monica, and Camilla were already invited and looking forward to it too.

"There's only one rule at my house, guys," Kate said.

No me, I thought.

"No talk about the next basketball game. We're in first place and we deserve to enjoy it!"

We're in first place? She had been on the team for one game and now she was part of the *we*. How did that happen? I ripped open my bag and took an angry bite of my sandwich. Without tasting it, I took another bite and another until I had nothing to take out my aggression on.

Camilla looked up from her ever-present iPod touch. "So, Kate, it must feel amazing to win your first game."

"That's an understatement. It was the best feel-ing. The kind you dream about, but that never really happens."

"Yeah, I have those dreams," Grace said. "Three sec-onds to go in the game. Championship on the line, screaming fans."

Monica jumped in. "I play it out every day on my driveway!"

"And all of you are so nice." Kate looked around the table. "My last team didn't eat lunch together or hang out."

That's because of me, I screamed silently. *I'm the one who made sure the team hangs out together!*

Kate was still talking. "Thank you for letting me be a part of the team in the middle of the season. You've all made me feel like I belong."

Holy cow! Was I the only one not seeing through all her baloney?

"My old team the Warriors played a good game, but a lot of the girls were mean. I didn't even like the coach."

"Well, we're glad to have you," Camilla said.

Even the subs were buying Kate's story. I couldn't take it anymore. I stood up to leave.

Jessie asked me, "Where are you going?"

"I said I forgot something in my locker, remember?" She nodded. I guessed my lame excuse was good enough for her.

It hurt to not feel comfortable at my own team's table. I had eaten lunch there every day for the last ... well, forever. I pushed my way into the hallway and bumped into Natalie. "I'm sorry, are you okay?"

"Yeah, I'm fine. Are you okay?"

"Uh-huh." I could barely put a word together in

response. Natalie looked like she didn't believe me.

I couldn't decide if I felt better or worse that I wasn't the only one not hanging on Kate like she was a rock star. "Why aren't you partying with Kate and the girls?"

"Had to ask for extra math help. Where are you going now?"

"I don't know."

"Can I come?"

I looked at her and thought, *Why do you want to hang out with me when you can be with rising-star Kate?* "I don't know . . ."

"Renna!" Jessie called from down the hall.

"I think when she invited me, she meant both of us," Jessie said kindly.

"No she didn't, Jessie. But thank you for thinking of me."

Natalie asked, "What are you talking about?"

I asked Natalie, "Can you give us a second?"

"Sure," she said, and turned away.

Jessie tried again. "Don't you think it's weird that Kate wouldn't invite the team captain?"

"Jessie, I don't know what to think anymore. I just don't care. The new girl doesn't have to like me or want to hang out with me just because I'm the captain." I started to walk away before tears burst from my eyes again. There was no way I was crying twice in the same lunch period.

"Well, if you're not going, then I'm not going."

"Don't do that. You should go, Jessie."

Jessie said, "I don't want to. If you're not good enough to be friends with, then neither am I."

"Is that supposed to be a compliment?"

"Yeah," she smiled.

I'm not sure how much I believed her. What grade seven doesn't want to go to the house of a grade eight? But I had an idea. "Just go to her house after school and report back to me. Tell me how it goes."

Jessie nodded. "See you at the game tonight."

Who knows, I thought. *Maybe, just maybe, everyone will have a horrible time and see Kate for what she really is.*

10 CAST OUT

Arriving at Maple Heights school alone for the game was bad enough. But to see nobody else on the basketball court was the kicker. Usually our team arrives early to warm up.

A teacher with a whistle and a couple of older kids entered the gym and started to set up. I asked for a ball and started to dribble it in front of a net. The echo of each bounce was another reminder that I was alone. I hoped everyone had had a horrible time at Kate's.

"You going to shoot?"

"Huh?"

Natalie had entered the gym so quietly I hadn't noticed. "Where is everyone?"

"You mean you weren't invited to the afterschool party?"

Natalie shook her head. "Whose party?"

"Kate's."

"Well, I'm always the last to know about these things. Besides, I don't like parties." She expertly ponytailed her hair with an elastic band.

"Oh." I held the ball, aimed it at the net, and fired. The ball hit the backboard and bounced left. *Figures.*

I heard the cackling of voices from outside the gym. It was Kate and the rest of the team. I opened the door and spotted Jessie at the back of the pack. "Hey, Jess."

"Renna. I missed you."

"Can we talk? I have some questions for you."

"Here?"

"Go get changed and meet me in the gym."

Back on the basketball court, Natalie was shooting hoops. On the wall was a large *Go Maple Heights Rockets* sign.

"So, can I bug you for some tips?" Natalie asked. "I really want to get more game time."

I wasn't in the mood. "Sure, but some other time."

I spotted Coach Philip, and tried to avoid him, but he made a beeline for me. "Hey, Renna. How are you?"

"I've been better."

He pulled out some water bottles and playbook papers. "Good."

"Good?"

"Oh, I'm sorry. Just a busy day at school. You know, things have been so busy we haven't had a chance to talk about how lucky we are."

"Lucky?"

"Yeah. Lucky to have Kate."

I wrinkled my eyes tightly. "How's that lucky?"

"Because we got such an amazing player. Caitlyn was great, and we could have been stuck with anybody when she left. But I think Kate's going to help us get to the playoffs! I know you're glad to see her finishing off all the hard work you've put into the team. "

I didn't know how to answer that. I turned in frustration toward Jessie, who had just hit the gym. "So how was it?"

"It was actually fun. We chatted online with a bunch of boys. You should have been there!"

"I wasn't invited, remember?"

Natalie was just standing there, looking at me expectantly.

"What?" I asked.

"Those pointers?"

"Not now, Natalie. We're talking."

"Oh, okay." She left.

"So, Renna," Jessie said. "Just ask Kate next time if you can come too. She's really easy-going."

"What planet are you from? She doesn't want me there."

"Pass." It was the voice I had come to dread. Kate was asking Natalie for the ball. Natalie passed it to her and we all watched Kate sink a long shot. Then she smiled at Jessie and walked over.

Jessie said, "So, Kate, next time you should invite Renna."

If I was a turtle and had a shell I would have sunk

my head into it. How could Jessie ask that? Lucky for me, Kate didn't get a chance to respond. The Rockets team emptied into the gym and jumped into their pre-game warm-up.

How could Jessie not see how much her attempt to force me into friendship with Kate hurt? I mean, had she even been listening to me?

Coach Philip called out, "Team huddle, everyone!"

I leaned in and wrapped my arms around Grace and Monica.

Grace said to me, "We missed you this afternoon."

I nodded. Directly ahead of me was Kate, and I locked eyes with her for a second. There is nothing like the stomach pain you get from staring your enemy in the eyes. The weird thing was that I had never had an enemy, unless you counted that boy in kindergarten who had poured glue in my hair.

Coach said, "I want everyone to have a good game and try your best. We're playing the last-place team, so go easy on them."

Everyone let out a hushed laugh.

Huddled in with my team, it brought back the pain of being alone all afternoon and having nowhere to go. Why didn't anyone ask, *Where's Renna?* Maybe they did and Kate told them that I couldn't make it.

"Let me hear, 'Go Hornets!'"

I gave a half-hearted cheer for the team. Before I knew it, the game was on.

The Rockets had the ball and I retreated to cover their point guard. They yelled out the play code, "Octopus Nine," but then nothing happened. I stayed with the point guard as she waited for a player to pass through. I could see her panic that the shot clock was counting down. She had ten seconds to try to score or we would get possession of the ball.

She called out another weird play, "Zebra Six."

Before I could react, the Rockets shooting guard zipped in front of me and blocked me from going anywhere. I turned to watch the point guard zip through traffic and lay it up. I should have been all over that one. The familiar voice of Coach Philip sprayed from the sidelines. "Let's go, Hornets!"

I dribbled the ball, waiting for that normal spark in my step. I don't know where it comes from, but this time I didn't feel it.

Grace chirped, "Open."

I flung the ball to her and she took it down the left side. She did a behind-the-back pass to Kate, who drove it to the net and scored. *Good for her. Like I care.*

The next time I brought the ball forward, I wondered if Kate treated a girl on her other team the way she was treating me. Maybe that's why she transferred teams. She was pushing around a girl on the Warriors and the coach kicked her off the team. I liked the idea. It meant that maybe she'd be kicked off the Hornets too. After bouncing from team to team, the league would probably notice and ban her from playing ball.

"Renna!"

Out of nowhere, a blue-and-white Rockets jersey flashed by me and took the ball from under my hands. One minute it was there, and the next it was in the basket. There were big smiles on the Rockets and disappointed frowns on the Hornets. I was embarrassed and speechless. I had lost track of what was happening in the game. That had never happened before.

"You okay out there?" Coach asked.

I nodded my head, still dazed by what happened.

"You want a timeout?"

"No . . . I'm okay."

"So what's it going to be, Coach?" The referee demanded.

"Ahh . . ."

Coach couldn't make up his mind so the referee made it for him. He blew his whistle and announced, "Timeout, Hornets."

I dragged myself to the sidelines where Coach was waiting for me.

"Are you okay?"

"Kinda."

"That doesn't sound good. Now, I don't claim to the expert here, Renna, but you're not using your left side. And the Rockets are seeing that. Know what I'm saying?"

"Uh-huh."

The subs crowded around, hoping this would be their chance to be picked. Like sharks, they smelled blood in the water.

Grace stepped up to face me. "Renna, you're not using the left side. Kate's open and you're not sending her anything."

Kate wants me to pass, I thought. *Fine.* I said, "I'll keep an eye out," with as much enthusiasm as I could muster.

"Okay, hurry up and get out there. Timeout's over." The Coach stopped for a second. "And try to make it look like you're having fun out there."

The ref blew his whistle and I let Grace take possession. She got backed into a corner, so I moved in to either pick her player or get the ball. The Rockets player was all over her, so I reached out my hands for the ball. I took it and yelled out, "Reset everyone," as I turned.

As my team got back into their normal positions, I looked for an open player. Emma couldn't break free, and Jessie was trying not to get called on a three-second time violation for being in the opposition's key. Kate was in the open. What option did I have?

"The shot clock!" Jessie warned.

I grabbed the ball and passed it high into Kate's corner. She jumped up and reached for it, barely getting contact with her fingertips. The ball continued out of bounds. The ref blew his whistle and pointed at our net, because it was Kate who lost our possession.

"Come on!" Kate grunted.

They wanted me to pass to her. Nobody said it had to be a good pass.

Grace slid by me, moving backward. "Come on, Renna. Get it together."

"You think you can do better?"

She stopped. "What? I didn't say that."

"I think you did. You think it's so easy . . . you take the point." I turned to the coach and yelled out, "Grace is taking the point."

He looked at me quizzically, but nodded anyway. Grace took the pass from Jessie and took two steps before passing it to me.

She jogged past me and said, "I never said I wanted to take over."

I thought about throwing it back to Grace, but that would be childish. It's not like I didn't want to win the game and keep our first-place spot. Besides, I had another option. At the half-court line I looked up to Kate, made eye contact, and shouted, "Switch pass!" Kate moved toward me and I moved toward her. When we met, I gave her the ball and took her position under the net.

Jessie immediately yelled, "Scramble!" I moved in and around the key, trying to shake my cover. I looked to Jessie with my right arm in the air, calling for the shot. When Jessie released the ball I could see it was off course.

My cover saw the same thing and alerted her team. "Rebound!"

I turned my back to the play and dug in, protecting my prime spot under the net. The ball was going to be mine. The ball appeared overhead and my eyes zeroed in on it as it hit the backboard, bounced off the rim, and leaped to the left. I followed the ball with my body, springing into action. The next thing I felt was a head-on-head collision. I dropped to the ground and landed hard on my knee. My head or my knee — what took pain priority? What had happened anyway?

I opened my eyes and winced. And saw Kate in the same position as I was in, on the floor. She rolled over and I could swear I saw a small smile on her face. That had been my ball and she knew it. How could she have slammed into her own teammate like that?

"You okay?"

I looked up to see the ref staring down at me. He and Coach Philip helped Kate and me to our feet. It was more of a struggle for me.

"Try to walk it off," Coach said.

I took one step and knew my knee was too bad to play. I hobbled to the bench while Kate shook off her pretend injuries.

Jessie was the first one by my side. "Are you all right? That was nasty."

"No, I'm not all right. It hurts."

Coach sent Camilla to get some ice. "You better

sit this out, Renna. Who should go on? What do you think?"

I knew that no one was more eager to sub in than Natalie. She peered over my shoulder, smiling encouragingly at me. But I was too uncomfortable and angry to be nice. "Whatever, I'm in pain."

"Umm . . . okay, Monica. You're up."

Natalie's smile vanish from her face. *Whatever*, I thought. *Join the club.*

Grace and Emma stopped by to check on me. It felt good to know they still cared, but it was too late. To say I was mad at Kate because my knee hurt was a definite understatement. *My life hurts!* I wanted to scream. Instead I looked up at Jessie and softly mouthed the words, "I quit."

11 WWW.RENNASLIFESUCKS.CA

After the knee injury, I got Coach to call my mom and bring me home. No point warming the bench without the possibility of playing. Staying home from school the next day was a must but, as the day dragged on, my bedroom seemed to grow smaller.

Around three, the phone rang.

"Hello?"

"Renna. It's Mom."

I could tell my mom was sitting at her office desk because she had her business voice on. "How are you doing?"

"I'm okay."

"Are you resting your knee?"

"Uh-huh." I didn't want to give her a full on *yes* because I had sort of stretched the truth with her. My knee had been really throbbing the night before, but when I woke up that morning it was somehow all better. I wanted my knee to be really hurt because it was my proof against the Beast. *See what she did to me? I* could tell people. *We're supposed to be on the same team!*

"Are you sure? I don't want you to make it worse."

I felt bad about not being honest with my mom, but I couldn't go back to school. I needed a break from the insanity of the team and my brainwashed team-mates. They all thought Kate was the best thing since Twitter, and only I knew how wrong they were. No matter how much I hinted at the bullying going on, they didn't seem to believe me.

"Poor girl. You must be so bored."

"Uh-huh." The sympathy felt good.

"So what are you up to?"

Let's see. I pretty much spent the morning seeing what my life would be like without basketball. I pulled a tennis racket out of a closet and smacked a ball against a cement wall in the basement. Tennis is good because it's not a team sport. There's no one to rely on. Too bad I was terrible. Then I picked up one of my dad's golf clubs and used it like a hockey stick, banging the tennis ball around. Again, not really my thing. "Well, I watched TV and made a sandwich."

"Do you want me to come home?"

I looked at the kitchen clock. In a few minutes school would be out. "Mom, I'm okay."

"Well, I love you and will take care of you tonight."

I could play hurt only for so long. Another second and I'd feel totally guilty. "Actually, it's starting to feel better already."

"That's because you're resting it. I'll see you in a bit."

"Bye." I hung up and looked around the empty house. A big part of me wanted to know if the team had won the game without me. Moving upstairs carefully — might as well keep the knee feeling better — I turned on the computer and waited for it to boot up. I double-tapped the shortcut icon to the league website, logged on, and opened the Hornets' page. I squinted at the screen, only half wanting to know.

"Let's see," I said to no one in particular. "We lost!" I stopped, surprised at the excitement in my voice. I felt sort of happy. If the team had won without me, then I was replaceable.

I spotted a blinking hyperlink on the bottom of the screen. It was a private message. I clicked on it and was surprised by what it read: *emag eht evael ot dah uoy dab oot*.

"What?" I stared at it, knowing it was coded. The word, *eht* caught my eye. I sounded it out, "E-h-t. What's an eht?" Next, I looked at *oot*. That didn't make any sense. It was like doing a math puzzle. So I wrote it down on a piece of paper. I started moving the paper around, wondering if it was a picture puzzle. When I flipped it all the way around, the word *oot* stood out again. It read: *too*. And *eht* read *the*. It was backward!

Excited that I had solved the puzzle, I read it out loud to myself: "Too bad you had to leave the game." Was that good or bad? It depended on how I read it.

As I was wondering who would be sending me

messages in code, another message popped up: *resol, tuo ti erugif.* "Figure it out, loser!" That had Kate all over it. It was a private message so no one else would see it. I couldn't even prove it was Kate, but it had to be. She was coding it and keeping it anonymous so I couldn't report her.

The blue *chat request* box opened up on the bottom right of my screen. Kate just couldn't leave it alone! I clicked to accept. The chat box grew bigger and I typed:

18 says… That coded post was stupid.

My fingers were moving faster than I could think.

18 says… When everyone finds out about you, you'll never play bball again.

The person on the other side typed:

16 says… Renna?
18 says… That's right.
16 says… It's Grace.
18 says… Oh, hey, Grace.

I was wrong! Kate was smarter than I thought. I was glad Grace couldn't see my embarrassment.

18 says… What's going on?

16 says… How's your knee?

18 says… It's better. I was really worried that when Kate hit me, I'd be out for the season with a shattered knee.

16 says… She hit you?

18 says… Oh yeah.

16 says… It looked more like an accident from where I was standing.

18 says… It was an intentional hit.

16 says… Whatever. Doesn't sound like something she'd do.

I shook my head, not that Grace could see me. But how could Grace understand, when she thought everyone was perfect?

18 says… How was school?

16 says… Okay. Someone here wants to say hi … Hey there, Renna.

18 says… Who's that?

16 says… It's M.

18 says… Hi, Monica.

16 says… Too bad you had to leave the game.

18 says… Thanks, but I'm doing better, Monica.

16 says… That's too bad too. It's not Monica, weirdo.

Weirdo? What?

16 says… Figure it out, resol?

There it was — *resol* … loser! A cold shiver ran down my back. The Beast was on the other side.

16 says… won pu evig

I read it backwards: "give up now." I was so furious I could have smashed my hand through the computer screen. I typed:

18 says… Not a chance.
16 says… Not a chance what?
18 says… Who's there now?
16 says… It's Monica, but that was Kate just being silly.

I felt my hands and jaw clench. Wherever I went, whichever direction I turned, I couldn't escape Kate. She was taking over my team, my friends, my life. I wanted to burst with anger. But I finally had some evidence. The chat could be proof. I searched my keyboard for the key to print screen. In health class, we learned how to print chats to battle cyberbullying. I never thought I'd need it. I found the key, but before I could print, another chat appeared.

16 says… GTG. LOL.

I quickly pushed the key, but the chat box closed down and disappeared. And so did any chance I had for stopping the Beast. Argh!

I ran downstairs into the basement and found the tennis ball. I whipped it at the wall, pretending Kate was standing in front of it, over and over again until I was sweaty and exhausted. I dropped down to the cement floor and soaked up its coolness. I couldn't figure out if I wanted to cry or scream.

12 THE MEETING

Grace and Emma were playing twenty-one on the school's outdoor basketball court. Grace took a shot, trying to get a three-pointer. The ball missed the net, so Emma picked up the rebound and put it in.

"What's the score?" I called out as I walked toward them.

Emma dribbled the ball and picked a new spot to shoot from. "Fifteen to twelve for Grace."

"Only because I've been nailing it from down-town," said Grace.

"Yeah," Emma said, "she's been sinking them."

I nodded my head. The school grounds were empty except for a half-dozen early drop-off students.

"So why are we meeting early?" Grace asked.

"You'll see," I said. "We have to wait for Jessie."

Emma dribbled the ball and picked it up for her shot. "Okay, this one's for fifteen and the tie." She tossed the ball in the air.

I yelled out, "It's a brick." I was right. The ball

bounced clumsily off the backboard and Grace had to chase it down.

"Oh, come on," Grace said, standing in line with the net. She had to sink it without a backboard to rely on.

"You can do it!" Emma encouraged her.

I watched Grace's ball go high, soaring over the net to Emma in the far corner.

"Three points," Emma called, catapulting the ball over her shoulder to the net.

The ball was long and wide from the start. I stepped in and caught it.

"Hey, that's mine!" Grace protested.

I frowned at Emma. "You take stupid shots like that out here and you'll end up doing the same thing in a game."

Emma flashed me a goofy smile, probably trying to figure out if I was joking. I wasn't. "We were just playing," said Emma as she saw how serious I was.

I mocked her, "We were just playing." I looked over at Grace. "Give me a break. At the end of the season, when we don't win the championship, remember this moment."

Before Grace could reply, a new voice broke in. "Hi, guys. Everything okay?" It was Jessie, at last.

"We were waiting for you. Come on." I walked with Grace's basketball off the painted court to the brick wall where our bags were.

"So why are we here?" Grace asked.

"Yeah, I could have slept in," Emma said, obviously still mad at me for trying to improve her game.

Not my problem if she can't handle the truth, I thought. I pulled the girls closer. "I wanted to have a meeting."

"What about the other girls?" Grace asked.

How predictable, I thought. *Always thinking about someone else*. "Well, this is important and I thought it would be best if just the starting line is here."

"Kate's in the starting line," Grace added.

It didn't even register because I had removed the name *Kate* from the dictionary in my brain. In its place was a blank. Nothing. A dead space.

"Are you quitting or something?" Emma asked.

"What? How can you say that?"

She shrugged.

I pushed for an answer. "How'd you hear that? Who said that?"

"No one. I don't know."

It's Kate, I thought. *Emma just doesn't want to admit it*. "I'm the captain and I'm not quitting. I called you here because I want to tell you something that the coach doesn't have the guts to say. We're not playing like we used to, and we're not going to make the playoffs."

"The coach said that?" Jessie asked.

"The reason is simple. Everyone's caught up in the drama of the new girl."

"You mean Kate," Grace clarified.

"Yes, I mean Kate," I responded. "I said this when

she joined and no one listened to me. She's a Warrior at heart and is fooling everyone into thinking that she wants the Hornets to win."

"Then why would she sink a winning bucket?"

"To look credible," I explained. This wasn't working the way I hoped it would. I tried another shot. "True or false. Were we stronger before she showed up?"

Jessie pointed. "Speaking of . . ."

I turned to see Monica walking toward our group, and with her was the Beast.

"You all look so serious," Monica said. "What are you talking about?"

Emma answered, "Oh, we were just having a meet —"

I cut her off. "We're just hanging out. What, is it against the law?"

The Beast smiled and said, "You should have let us know." I was barely listening.

"Didn't you get Renna's e-mail for the team meeting?" Emma asked.

How could Emma say that? But I didn't care. It made me feel good to let the Beast know what it feels like to be left out.

"No, I didn't get her e-mail."

"I only sent it to the e-mail addresses I have," I said the same way the Beast talked to me — no eye contact and no response.

"Oh. No big deal."

I surprised myself by saying, "Give your e-mail

address to me." I could do a lot of things with her e-mail.

She responded, "Just let Jessie forward it to you. Jessie, you have it, right?"

Jessie nodded, trying not to look at me.

My best friend has the Beast's e-mail address? They've been e-mailing behind my back? I had to say, "Wouldn't want you to miss another team gathering." Before she could respond, I added, "But the coach gave you a password to the team website, right?"

"Yeah."

That's how she posted those backward shots at me. "Well, if you really need to e-mail me," I turned to Jessie, "Jessie can forward my address to you."

I turned and walked away. My mission was accomplished — make Kate feel left out and let the girls know where I stand. They needed to know that Kate is the problem.

"Hey, Renna." Jessie stopped me when I was almost at the school doors.

"Don't worry about the e-mail thing," I told her. "I'll get over it."

"I wasn't worried," Jessie said angrily. "I was shocked at how you talked to Emma when she missed that shot on the basket." Jessie had one hand on her hips and the other one pointing at me. You're not the coach and Emma can do what she wants out here. If we don't win the championship, you can't tell her it's all her fault."

"But it's the truth."

"That's no excuse."

Now I was pointing at *her*. "Jessie, you used to be all about winning too."

"But I was never mean about it. *You* were never mean about it. I don't know what happened to you, but you're acting like a jerk."

"Now's a great time to care what happened to me. What happened to *you*? Oh, let me guess."

"Guess what?" Jessie asked.

"Why don't you just go and e-mail your new best friend."

***

Getting my homework out of my desk and into my stuffed backpack would have been easier if Natalie wasn't pestering me.

"It's just that I can't make the shot when I don't have a backboard. That's when my shot sucks."

I thought about shooing her away like a pesky fly buzzing around my ear. Then I thought of a better idea. "You know, Natalie, that's the one thing separating *you* from *us* on the starting line."

"Really?"

"Yeah. If you can only shoot head-on into the net, instead of being able to sink it from around the key, the coach won't start you."

The Meeting

She stamped her foot like a frustrated child. "So how do I get better at it?"

A big idea fired in my head. If I could get Natalie's game up to speed, maybe I could somehow get her to replace Kate on the front line. That *somehow* was a big one, and I didn't know if Natalie had the right stuff.

"So you'll help me?" Natalie pleaded.

"Here's what you need to do when shooting from the bottom of the key. You need to send the ball up in the air. It has to arc up."

"Arc?"

"Yes." I went to the whiteboard and grabbed a marker. I could hear Mrs. Sherbet in the next classroom talking to a teacher, so I popped the cap off the marker and drew a stick person and a net. Then I connected the two with a high arc, a curve like the top of a rollercoaster. "If you don't give your shot enough height, if you line-drive it, it won't flop down into the net."

"But the distance is hard to judge."

"You just have to practise." I grabbed the small school garbage can — they resized the cans so we could become an eco-school — and grabbed some paper from the white recycling bin. "Might as well start now." I walked Natalie back behind some desks, crumpled a piece of paper, and handed it to her. "Arc it."

"Okay." She studied it like it was a game-winning shot and released it. The paper dropped short.

"Try it again. But you have to arc it up high." I crumpled another piece of paper and tossed it to her. She didn't shoot it. "What's wrong?"

"The net's usually a lot higher."

"Okay." I picked up the garbage and held it up above my head.

"Can I shoot?"

"You can arc. Go."

Natalie released the paper. It shot over the tiny garbage can and bounced off my forehead.

"Sorry."

I nodded.

Natalie took another shot. The scrunched-up paper hit the top of my head. The amazing thing was that she almost landed it. Too bad my head wasn't the net.

Maybe Natalie wasn't the right person for getting Kate off the team. "Keep trying," I sighed.

She reached for another piece of recycled paper.

"Not now," I said. "On your own time." I dropped the garbage can and pulled on my backpack with two hands. I needed a Plan B.

13 TWO-ON-TWO

Natalie followed me out of the classroom. I stopped just past the door when I saw Jessie with her hand on Emma's shoulder. It was hard to tell, but it looked like Jessie was consoling Emma.

"What's going on?" Natalie asked them.

"Not much," Emma said.

"Yeah, Emma and I are going to shoot some baskets," Jessie announced, without looking at me.

That's great, I thought. *How many enemies can I make?*

"Well, Natalie and I were just about to do the same, so you should join us."

Emma backpedalled. "Actually . . ."

"Come on," Natalie urged, "Renna was just giving me some pointers and I want to try them out."

"Yeah," I smiled, looking at Emma, "we can all use some pointers."

I grabbed the basketball beside Emma's backpack and walked outside. "So let's do two-on-two."

"Yeah," Natalie piped in excitedly. "Me and Renna

against the two of you."

"Actually, me and Emma against the two of you," I corrected her.

Emma waved me off, trying to get out of it. But Jessie looked down at me from her full height and said, "Bring it on."

I passed the ball hard to Jessie. She wasn't expecting it and fumbled it.

"Let's go," Jessie said. She threw the ball back to me, trying to catch me off guard, but I caught it.

I jumped into action. "Emma, go left." Emma ran to the left side, cut in and then forward, obeying each of my orders. Jessie approached me with her knees bent and arms spread wide. I spotted Emma, who had freed herself from Natalie, but I couldn't get her a good pass. Instead, I faked left and moved right around Jessie, who reached over me and smacked the ball out of my hands. The ball bounced and I got my hands on it just as Jessie did. "Foul!"

"It's our ball!" she demanded, pulling on it.

"You touched my hand, it's a foul." I yanked on the ball, trying to pry it free.

Natalie stepped forward, trying to end the tug of war. "Jessie, just give it to them."

"Fine."

The moment Jessie released the ball, I was flung backward and stepped over the painted white line.

"Out of bounds! Now it's ours," Jessie said. She

took the ball and quickly passed it to Natalie.

I shouted out to Emma, " Cover her!"

Natalie ran herself into a corner and had to take a no-backboard shot. Although the ball arced up, it missed the net. Emma tracked it down.

"Pass it!" I got the ball from Emma and deked around Jessie. I did a very smooth layup. It was in! I spun around and high-fived Emma. She smiled at me for the first time that day.

Jessie said, "Let's go, Natalie. Bring it out."

I passed Emma and said, "Switch." As I moved in on Natalie, she got scared and made a bad pass. I intercepted it and brought the ball into the key. A very frustrated Jessie was coming, so I did a drop pass to Emma, who was waiting under the net. The ball went into her hands and then, somehow, out of her hands and out of bounds.

"Come on!" I complained.

"I'm sorry," said Emma. Her smile was gone.

"Sorry is not good enough. I set you up with an open shot."

"I did my best." She stopped and pointed. "Look."

I turned to see Jessie and Natalie bringing up the ball.

"Just cover Natalie," I told Emma. I moved in on Jessie, who was already at the top of the key. She lined up for a three-pointer and, when she jumped, so did I. Since Jessie was taller, she got it over my head and in.

Jessie passed me the ball. "Looks like you're down by one."

I called Emma over. "Get under the net for a pass or a rebound."

"Okay." She didn't sound too confident.

"Do you want to bring the ball forward?"

"No."

"Then get into position."

I took my time dribbling the ball, giving Emma time to get ready. I pushed my back into Jessie and dribbled the ball as far away from my body as possible. I nudged Jessie backward, turned around, and moved toward the net. Immediately, Natalie moved in on me, and the two of them double-teamed me. I had no shot or pass. As Jessie and Natalie tried to swat the ball from my hands, I lobbed it up and over them, using my right arm as a catapult.

The ball headed toward Emma, who had the entire net to herself. The ball hit the ground and bounced high. Emma mistimed her jump, and the ball leaped over her and out of bounds. I couldn't take it anymore. "What are you doing? How can you do that?" I yelled.

"I'm sorry, Renna," Emma said meekly. "I'm doing my best and that wasn't a great pass."

Jessie interrupted. "Stop arguing and let's play."

I wasn't done. "That's two open nets that you missed, Emma. What happened to your game? You used to be good."

Emma turned away from me. I could see that she was crying. I had a tingling sensation like I had just done something horrible. I didn't know what to do.

Emma turned around, her face full of tears. "You're a terrible captain!" she shouted at me. And then she ran off. Natalie followed her.

Jessie pointed at me, and said furiously, "Look what you did! How could you do that?"

I stood frozen and confused.

Jessie persisted. "What's your problem?"

"You don't understand how it feels to be me right now."

"How it feels to be you? What about how it feels to be Emma? You bullied her this morning and again today."

"I am not a bully!"

"'Everyone could use some pointers.' Those weren't pointers. It was victimization." Jessie took a big breath.

"I'm not a bully."

"You're acting like one."

"I'm the one being bullied!"

That stopped Jessie short. "Who's bullying you?"

I realized how loudly I was talking. "Kate," I whispered.

"What?"

"Yes, Kate. When nobody else is around. She's been physically pushing me, badmouthing me, sending me nasty coded messages, and making me feel terrible about myself and my life."

"Really? Why didn't you tell me?"

I slapped my hands against my legs. *What!?* "I *tried* to tell you."

"I'm sorry, Renna. When did this happen?"

"From the moment I said hi to her."

I was surprised how good it felt to tell someone. And then I started to feel bad. I played the moment with Emma over in my mind and realized how much of a jerk I was being. I had been verbally abusing her, acting like a bully . . . like Kate. I covered my face and wanted everything, including Jessie, to just disappear.

14 OUT IN THE OPEN

"I don't want to apologize. I'm too embarrassed," I told Jessie.

"You have to. You don't want to be a bully, right?"

"Jessie, I'm not a bully."

"Did you say mean things to Emma?"

I nodded.

"Was it a one-time thing or repeat?"

I didn't want to say it. "Repeat."

"Then you're a bully by definition."

"But, but —"

"Is Kate a bully?"

"For sure."

"Did she say mean things to you?"

"Yes, but she also pushed me."

"Doesn't matter."

"I am not like Kate. No way."

"You're right, the one thing that bullies never do is apologize. That's why you're going to."

I liked this angle. Anything to get the bully label off

me. "So, if I apologize, I'm no longer a bully?"

"Yes." Jessie pointed. "And there's your victim."

The word *victim* made me cringe. It made it sound like I committed a crime or something. I stood, frozen, the same way I did when Kate first pushed me. The thought of being a bully, being anything like Kate, scared me.

That fear that comes with being bullied had kept me up at night. It had left a very bad taste in my mouth, sort of like metal. My mom had bugged me about not eating dinner, but how could I have eaten with that taste in my mouth? My dad had bugged me about not wanting to play twenty-one on the driveway. And they'd both thought I was sick. I was exhibiting flu symptoms: no energy, dry mouth, hot to the touch. Now I couldn't get the image of Emma crying out of my head. I had been a jerk to someone I cared about.

Jessie interrupted my sulking. "Remember what you told me when I was too scared to present my All-About-Me poem in grade three?"

"No."

"You said, 'Do it!'"

"I said that? Doesn't sound too inspiring."

"Well, it was for me. Do it, and it's over."

"I'm scared."

Jessie just looked at me and pointed toward Emma.

"How come you know so much about all this?" I asked, trying to stall.

"I paid attention in health class."

"Oh, right."

Jessie grabbed my hand and started to drag me toward Emma. I stopped her.

"What now?" she said.

"So this means we're best friends again?"

"Yes. Now, come on."

When we got to Emma, I froze up again.

"What's up, Jessie?" Emma asked.

"Renna wants to talk to you."

"Oh. I don't know . . . only if you stay."

Jessie nodded and stepped out of the way so I could start.

The words, *do it and it's done*, ran through my head. Suddenly I blurted out, "I'm so sorry, Emma. I never meant to hurt you, it's just that my life sucks right now and I took it out on you, but I was stupid to do that because you're such a nice person." I stopped and took a big breath. "Emma, I'm a bully."

Emma looked at me quizzically. "You are?"

"And I need to apologize to you so I'm not a bully anymore."

"Okay."

"I'm sorry for all the mean things I said to you. I put you down and I made you feel bad, maybe because I was feeling bad and I'm sorry. Sorry. Sorry. Sorry."

Emma looked at me and smiled.

Jessie smiled. "That wasn't so hard, was it?"

"But doesn't she have to accept my apology for this to work?" I asked, desperate.

Emma stepped forward and hugged me. "I accept. Thank you for admitting the truth."

I said, "You're welcome," happy that I had Emma back as a friend. "I think I got on your case because Kate was being so mean to me."

Talking it out, I felt a whole lot of guilt drain from my body. I felt ten pounds lighter.

"Hold on, Renna," Emma said. "Kate's been bullying you?"

"It's no excuse for the way I have been treating people, but it's the truth."

"What did she do?"

"Let's see — pushed me into the lockers, triped me, talked meanly to me, kept me from hanging out with my friends, and left nasty messages for me online."

Jessie turned to me. "I guess you tried to tell me, Renna, but I had no idea."

I nodded, holding back tears. There was no way I was going to cry.

"So the big question is," Emma said, "what are you going to do about it?"

"Nothing. Learn to hide better, maybe."

"You can't do that," said Emma.

Jessie repeated, "You can't do that."

Emma said, "Confront your bully."

What? "It's not that easy. I can't just go up to Kate

and start a conversation."

Jessie leaned in. "Do it!"

"Nice try, Jessie, but it's not that easy."

"Well, if you're not going to confront her," Emma began, "then you better hope she slips up and someone else sees it. Like a teacher. Teachers have to report bullying when they see it."

"You're brilliant, Emma!"

"I am?"

I jumped up and down a little, clapping my hands. "Yes. All I have to do is trap Kate into bullying me in front of a teacher."

Jessie asked: "Kate's in grade eight. How are you going to get her and Mrs. Sherbet in the same spot at the same time?"

"I don't," I said. "I'll get her to slip up in front of Coach! He's a teacher. Will you help?"

"I will." Emma nodded.

"I will too." Jessie smiled. "Anything to get my best friend back to normal."

15 GAME PLAN

The big basketball game at our school was in a half-hour, but I didn't care. I was too busy thinking of how great it would feel to have someone catch Kate in action. Coach's eyes would bulge and he'd lay into her, kicking her off the team and banning her from playing basketball in the Richmond Hill area for life. The next time I'd probably see Kate would be when she comes to the Air Canada Centre to watch me play for the Raptors.

The change-room door opened so suddenly I almost jumped. It was Emma.

"Jessie's gone to get the coach and Kate's warming up with Grace," she reported.

"Okay." The plan sounded so good when we made it, but now I wasn't so sure.

"You ready for this?"

"No, but I have nothing to lose."

"Good luck."

"Thanks."

I opened the door leading to the court and spotted Kate and Grace warming up, shooting hoops. I picked up a basketball and started to dribble it toward them.

"What's happening, Renna?" Grace asked.

"Not much." Before I could take my first shot, Emma appeared at the front doors.

"Hey, Grace, can I ask you something?"

"Sure, what's up?"

"Uh . . . actually I need to show you something. Do you have a second?"

Grace took aim and fired a shot into the net. "Sure. I'll be back, Kate."

It was just me on the court with Kate, alone with the Beast. One-on-one for the first time. I took a shot from inside the key and sunk it. Retrieving my ball, I glanced at the big door at the entrance and the two smaller side doors on the other side. No sign of Jessie and the coach. Nothing. *It's too early to worry*, I told myself.

Kate swooshed her shot into the net and I did the same, in some sort of weird silent competition. My third ball went in with very little difficulty. But Kate's ball took an ugly spin off the rim and clattered to the ground. I held in my smile. Kate picked up her ball and stepped in front of me before I could take my next shot.

"Can't wait to rip that captain's C off your jersey and put it on mine," she said nastily.

I stood my ground and eyed the door, hoping the coach would appear.

Kate turned around and took another shot. She missed short.

This time my smile was so wide she could see it from across the court. I wanted to push her on, get her so that when the coach entered he'd see something real. Something big.

"You may think you're great," said Kate. "But the problem is you either have it or you don't. See, I was born with it. And you don't have it." Kate lined up another shot and this time sank it. "See what I mean?"

I picked up my ball and looked up at the net, half my mind lining up my shot and half my mind praying to the basketball gods for the coach to show up. I pulled back and released the ball with too much spin. It hit the backboard, then the rim, and bounced wildly to the left.

The stupid ball rolled back to Kate and slowed right in front of her. I had to get right up to her to pick it up and, as I grabbed for it, she swung her foot around and kicked it away. When I looked up she was smiling down at me. I didn't move, but I eyed her ball like I was going to grab it. But instead of taking her ball, once more I looked to the doors. Where was Jessie with Coach?

"Why do you keep looking at the door?"

"No reason." If there was an abort button on this stupid mission I would have pushed it.

Just then, the door opened, and Coach and Jessie entered.

Before I could even stand up, Kate stepped back and screamed, "Stop bugging me! Ever since I joined this team you've been doing everything to get me to leave!"

She tore to the far corner of the basketball court and broke out in major tears. I turned to Jessie and Coach, wide-eyed and stupefied. I had tried to play Kate, but she did it to me even worse!

Coach looked at me, frowning. For the first time ever, he used his teacher voice on me. "Renna?"

Before I could plead my case, both teams poured onto the court. I stepped toward Coach, looking at Jessie. She peeked through her fingers to see how he would react.

"Renna," said Coach sternly, "I thought you had good character. You've always treated people with respect. I'm going to have to look into this, and —" He didn't finish his thought, but I knew where he was heading. "Don't think about playing tonight."

I did the only thing I had become good at — hiding. I shot off toward the locker room. Not crying was not an option, so as soon as I got to the empty change room, I let it out.

Jessie entered. "Renna, just calm down."

"Calm down? I was just kicked off the team!"

"No you weren't."

Jessie sat down beside me. "We'll figure something out."

"No, it's over. I'm done playing for this stupid team. Let Kate have it!"

"Renna, you're not a quitter. I tried my best to get Coach into that gym sooner, but he was on his phone. I was practically jumping up and down, but he wouldn't get off the phone. I'm sorry."

"It's not your fault." My crying finally stopped and we sat in silence for a few seconds. Finally, I could speak. "I can't believe this."

"We'll set up Kate again."

"There's no point. With me off the team, there's nothing to get back at Kate for."

"What about for ruining your life?"

"I can't prove it."

The door swung open and Emma appeared. "Are you okay?"

"I've been better," I admitted.

"There's only one option now," Emma said.

"Change schools?" I said hopefully.

Emma bent down in front of me. "No. Confront her."

"No way."

"Emma's right," said Jessie. "You have nothing to lose. Don't let her win."

I nodded my head. I stood up with no intention of really walking out there. For the first time I wondered if, somehow, I had brought this on myself. Could I be to blame?

Emma stood next to me as Jessie pushed the door open. I moved through it, my legs outrunning my dwindling courage. In the crowded space of the gym, I found a path to Kate between both teams warming up. As I watched, she made a basket, fetched her ball, and lined up again behind Monica for another shot. As I pushed myself toward her, the rest of the gym turned blurry. It felt like all the air was being sucked out through a crack in a wall, leaving the entire inside a vacuum. No air, no noise. Just the feeling of my heart bursting through my rib cage. I arrived at Kate at the same time as she turned around.

"What do *you* want, capt'n?"

"I need to talk to you."

"You mean like, about boys and makeup? Or about how much you suck?"

Monica gave Kate a surprised and ugly look, the kind of look you give someone after they fart.

I thought seriously about backing off, but my feet wouldn't move.

"Well it's been a fascinating talk," said Kate airily. "We should do this again sometime, but right now I've got a basketball game to win."

I turned to leave, but saw Jessie and Emma hovering behind me like two guardian angels. I spun around and caught Kate off guard. A rush of emotions buried and backlogged inside of me escaped.

"You really hurt me," I said in as loud a voice as I

could muster. "I tried to be nice to you, and all you did was push me away. I didn't ask for a new player on the Hornets and I certainly didn't ask for one who would physically hurt me or leave nasty messages for me on-line or say mean things to my face and try to scare me from showing up at school or basketball games, one who would turn all my friends against me. But you did that to me and you made me feel bad about my-self, even though I didn't do anything mean to you." I stopped and realized I needed to breathe.

Kate stood motionless, surrounded by accusations. Besides the odd squeaking of shoes on the court floor, the gym was silent, and all eyes were on us, even those of the coach from the other team.

Coach Philip left the bench and made a beeline toward me.

"Renna, what's going on?"

"Coach, I don't know what she's talking about," Kate said. Her face started to turn red.

I ignored Coach and stayed focused on Kate. "You pushed me, you said nasty things to me . . ." My eyes filled with tears that reached the brink of my eyelids. I didn't know if I could keep the dam from cracking. "You bullied me!"

Kate kept her focus on the coach. "Coach, you saw what happened before — she's the bully!"

"That's a lie!" I shouted.

"Now I don't know what's going on or who to

believe," Coach Philip said, shoving his fingers through his hair. "Bullying is a serious issue and I don't want it on my team. Both of you better sit out tonight."

"Coach," I pleaded. "You have to believe me. I wouldn't lie to you."

"And I would lie?" asked Kate.

I looked around and noticed that the whole team had gathered around us.

"We will just have to deal with this after the game," said Coach sadly. "I think both your parents will have to be involved."

Mr. Clarkson, the English teacher who was acting as referee, turned to our team. "Coach, please send someone for the tipoff." The opposition were ready and in position.

"Please give me two minutes," said Coach Philip. "This is serious."

I couldn't believe what was happening. I finally had the guts to announce that I was being bullied, and Kate was making people suspect me.

Jessie stepped forward. "Coach, what Renna is saying is true."

Grace stepped forward for Kate. "What proof do you have, Renna? You can't accuse someone without proof."

What could I say? I didn't have any proof. Kate was getting away with it.

The other team's coach yelled out, "Ref, that's a delay of game."

The referee turned back to us. "Coach, the game's starting. Are the Hornets forfeiting?"

"One more minute, please," the coach pleaded. "Girls, we have to —"

"I have proof." It was Natalie.

She stepped forward with her head down. "Kate has been bullying me too. Leaving threatening messages for me on the team website."

Natalie stood by me as all eyes turned to Kate. It wasn't just her word against mine anymore. It would take a lot of shovelling to get herself out of this one.

I turned to Natalie and was surprised to recognize the hurt in her eyes, the same hurt I'd been keeping to myself. The same hurt I had seen in Emma. All this time and I had no idea.

"Renna, I was getting around to telling you," Natalie said. "You know, because you're team captain."

"Well, I think I was too wrapped up in my own stuff to notice."

"Well, Kate," Coach Philip said, "I'm shocked."

"Is it true?" Grace asked Kate, who stood alone facing Natalie and me, her victims.

Kate bowed her head and nodded. Then she bolted out of the gym.

Coach turned to the referee. "Ref, I'm sorry, but we have to forfeit the game. Team issues."

The last thing I wanted was for the whole team to suffer for what was going on. By forfeiting the game, we put our first-place position in jeopardy. I didn't know how to feel. Finally everyone knew about Kate, but things didn't seem to be better.

16 BULLY, BYSTANDER, VICTIM

As soon as I convinced Coach Philip to start the game without us, I surprised everyone, including myself, when I took off after Kate. I was chasing my bully. I caught up with her just outside the gym doors, where students were selling popcorn and colourful sports drinks.

"What do you want from me?" Kate asked. "Haven't you made me look bad enough?"

"I want to know why," I said. And it surprised me that I really did.

"Don't worry about it."

I looked directly into her eyes. "Because of where my family is from? Is that why?"

"No! I'm not a racist!" Kate looked away from me, but then turned right back. "You don't understand . . . you won't understand."

"Try me."

"Better to be tough than a target," Kate mumbled.

"I don't get it." I was confused. What target was she talking about? "Kate, you have to do better than that."

"Because I was bullied!" she exploded. She slapped her hands against her legs. "Okay? I was bullied. And my life was horrible because of it, and when I came here, I guess I expected the worst."

"You were bullied? Then why go after —" I stopped in midsentence because I knew the answer to the question I was asking. Kate bullied me for the same reason I bullied Emma. I took my frustration out on Emma because Kate was taking her frustration out on me. It didn't make what I did right, and it wasn't an excuse . . . but it happened and now I knew why it happened.

"Renna, you practically jumped on me when I arrived," said Kate. "Telling me your life story and showing me how to fit right in. You also let me know who was the boss of the whole team — you. It's like I had to be best friends with you, or I would get kicked off the team."

She had a point. Maybe I had come on a little strong. "Yeah, I don't think of anything but what the team needs. Maybe I was being less of a captain and more of a —"

"Team owner?"

That was a good one. I felt a grin creep across my face.

I laughed.

Then we both smiled.

After a pause, Kate said in a small voice, "I'm sorry, Renna. I guess I just assumed that I would be bullied again if I didn't strike first."

"So, Kate, who bullied you?"

"Does it matter?"

"Yeah, it really does."

"Don't laugh, but it was my team captain."

"The captain of the Warriors?"

"Yep. Number 11."

Kate turned like she was about to leave. "And now you know why I moved schools."

"Really?"

"Yes. It was that bad."

"Why didn't they just suspend her?"

Kate said, timidly, "Because I couldn't prove it."

So Kate had run away from the problem, just like I had wanted to the whole time. But there was a way she could feel better about it, just like I finally did.

"Do you know who we're playing in, like, five minutes?" I asked.

Kate nodded. "The Warriors. I'm glad I don't have to face them."

"But you have to."

"Give me one good reason."

"You have to confront your bully."

***

The basketball game was already in play, but our return to the gym brought all Hornet eyes on us. We scurried to the bench next to Coach and sat down, trying not to distract the players on the court.

"What's happening, girls?" asked Coach.

I spoke first. "Everything's okay. Please don't suspend Kate."

Kate smiled. "Yeah, we've worked out our similarities."

I grinned.

"What about the bullying?

"It's over."

"We'll still have to talk about it."

"That's okay," I said.

"So tomorrow at lunch in my classroom?"

Kate and I nodded.

"Great," Coach said, "I thought I lost both of you. Okay, I'm subbing you in right now."

But Kate had another apology to make before we could play as a team. "No, wait, Coach," I said. "Can you give this line a few more minutes? They're doing really well."

"Whatever you say. You are my assistant coach."

"Actually," I said, feeling an odd sort of relief. "I'm just the captain. I'll leave the coaching to you."

I sat on the bench next to Kate and watched the game play. Natalie, subbing in my position as point guard, managed to blow past her aggressive cover and passed the ball to Monica, who drove it to the net for a layup. I stood up and clapped as loud as I could, showing my support. Natalie looked back at me and smiled.

The Warriors returned, attacking our net in a full-court press. They lined up for a three-pointer and sunk it just as the halftime buzzer sounded. When the ball landed in Monica's hands, Coach Philip stood up and yelled, "Time!"

The Hornets emptied off the court and we all gathered around Coach.

Natalie wiped well-earned sweat off her face. "What's up, Coach?"

I handed Natalie a bottle of water. "Well, you're playing really well out there," said Coach. "But there's something important someone needs to say. Kate?"

"Coach, we're in the middle of a game!" Monica complained.

"This one's important," I said.

Kate cleared her throat. "I want to apologize to Natalie. I said and did a lot of bad things, and I'm sorry."

Natalie looked warily at Kate. "And things are good between you and Renna?"

Kate nodded.

Coach rolled up his sleeves. "Okay. Now the air is cleared. We're not going to win this one unless we start communicating. Talk to each other, make it happen." He opened his clipboard and flipped through the papers. "Now, let's see . . ." Suddenly, he closed his clipboard, threw it to the floor, and said, "Have fun and do your best."

I nodded. For the first time I could remember, Coach sounded like a coach.

"Anything to add?" he asked me.

"Coach, I think you said it best."

"Good. Natalie, you and your line are playing very well, but you need to rest if you're gonna go out again, so first line's going on. Let's go, girls! Let's win this one!"

17 REBOUND

I slapped hands with Natalie and hit the court. By the time I was in position, the referee had blown his whistle, and Jessie threw the ball to me from the sidelines. It felt good to hold the ball again, to bring it to half court with all the Hornets looking at me, waiting for me to make the play.

"Come on everyone, I can't hear you!" Coach said we needed to communicate.

Instantly, I heard the team call out. Jessie was going in and out of the key to escape the three-second violation. "I'm open!" she shouted. Emma was performing amazing cuts, running back and forth, trying to lose her cover. I looked to Kate and spotted her doing the same thing on the other side.

The Warriors point guard attempted to slap the ball from my hands. "Come on losers," she said. "Make a play already."

I stared back at her and yelled out, "Someone give me a pick!" Kate stepped forward, then hesitated. Emma stepped in and provided me with the perfect pick that allowed to skirt around the Warriors player.

I headed into heavy traffic around the net. Looking up, I saw Jessie being double-teamed under the net. Kate stood buried by a Warriors cover except for one hand that rose above her opponent's head. About to get pummelled by hands and fingers, I passed the ball sideways and it landed on Kate's hand. I completed the play by moving in to pick off her defender as she drove the ball hard to the net and slammed it in. I turned to celebrate, but stopped when the ref blew his whistle.

Kate looked back at me. "What did I do?"

"Foul, Number 23 defence," called the ref.

"Nothing. You're going to the free-throw line for two! Nice going," I told her.

"Okay."

"What's wrong?" I noticed Kate eyeing Warriors Number 11, the loud-mouth point guard. The letter C was stitched on the shoulder of her jersey. "She's the one?"

"Uh-huh."

The ref called Kate to the free-throw line and I positioned myself facing Number 11. "You can do it, Kate," I said.

"Funny," Number 11 said, "when she played for us she couldn't." She turned to Kate. "Remember how much you sucked?"

I felt horrible for Kate as she bounced the ball repeatedly before lifting and releasing it. It had a good arc, but it hit the rim and bounced away.

"See what I mean?" sneered Number 11.

I wanted to let Number 11 have it, but this was not my battle to fight.

Kate released another shot and it strayed left.

"That's okay," I said. "Good try, Kate." I wanted to tell Kate to confront this girl, even though we were in the middle of a game, but she had to find her chance.

The Warriors brought the ball into our zone and I did everything in my power to steal that ball from Number 11. She managed to get by me but, just before she attempted a three-pointer, I made contact with the ball and it rolled into a herd of players. Players struggled for the ball and I waited for it to pop out. The ref was raising his whistle to his lips as Grace jumped up with the ball.

The ball was ours and we had the Warriors off guard. I got the ball and, as much as I wanted to alley-oop it to Jessie running down the court, I knew we couldn't win the game that way. "Slow it down, take your positions," I shouted. In Warrior territory, no one could get free, so I called, "Scramble!"

The scramble confused the Warriors, but still I didn't have anyone to pass to. I decided to drive the ball down the middle to take a respectable, guaranteed layup. I faked left to lose Number 11 and dribbled hard toward the net. As I lifted off my right foot for the layup, Number 11 bodychecked me with her shoulder and I crashed to the ground. I cringed in pain and rolled over onto my back with my eyes closed.

I could hear Kate's voice. "You can't do that to my friend."

"Well, at least I'm not a traitor." That was Number 11.

"Well, at least I'm not a bully."

I opened my eyes enough to see Kate and Number 11 facing each other down, and when Mr. Clarkson, the ref, appeared I quickly closed them. The stop in play was giving Kate the moment she needed to confront her bully and I would stay "hurt" to give her as much time as I could.

The ref looked down at me. "Are you okay?"

I opened my eyes, squinting. Kate was still talking, so I stayed down.

"You bullied me from the moment I joined the Warriors."

Mr. Clarkson looked over at them. "So, your problem is that I just heard that. And as a teacher, I have to report it." He blew his whistle. "Warriors Number 11, that's five personal fouls. Have a seat, you're out of the game. Two shots from the free throw line, Hornets Number 18."

Jessie helped lift me up onto my feet. "Are you okay?" she asked.

"Bruised, but okay." I turned to the ref and said, "I don't think I can make the two shots. I need to sit down."

"Okay, then we'll have someone else do it."

I looked at Kate.

Kate nodded. She seemed confused and happy at the same time, with a large dash of relief thrown in. "Why are you helping me so much?" she asked me. "After what I did to you?"

"Remember? I know what it's like to be bullied."

"You know, I feel really bad about that."

"Don't worry about it. I can see what you had to go up against. Feels good to confront, huh?"

"Yes. Especially after hiding for so long."

The ref put the ball in Kate's hands.

As I headed to the bench, I turned to Kate. "So, there's one thing you can do for me."

"What?"

My brain ran through all the things I wanted to say, things I was used to saying — make those two baskets, get us back into first place, Balance–Elbow–Extend–Follow-through.

Instead I took a deep breath and said, "Go, Hornets!" It felt great to be back.

ACKNOWLEDGEMENTS

This book would not have been possible without the help of many people I have the good fortune of knowing. Many thanks to Carrie Gleason at Lorimer for her guidance in the development of Fadeaway and to Kat Mototsune for her editing expertise. Kat helped me get down on paper the kind of story I had in my mind. Lynn Bennett, my agent, thank you for the time you've spent with me helping me to understand the ever-changing publishing world.

Thank you to Philip, my wonderful grade five student who bravely lent his name to the coach character. And to Robert Hynd, a phenomenal teacher and basketball coach who let me ride along as his assistant and take incessant notes on everything he did and said. This seems like the right time to tell you both that the bumbling coach in this book is me.

MORE SPORTS, MORE ACTION
www.lorimer.ca

Slam Dunk
By Steven Barwin

Mason's basketball team, the Cabbagetown Raptors, is going co-ed after seven successful seasons. He's pretty open-minded about the change, especially after he meets Cindy, a really top-notch player. The other guys aren't so sure. Before long everyone has taken sides, the Raptors' chances of making the national finals are in jeopardy.

SK8ER
By Steven Barwin

Jordy Lee and his friends spend all their free time on their skateboards, navigating the crowded streets of Toronto's Kensington Market. They're thrilled when a new skateboarding park opens and offers a youth competition with a rich prize. The talented Alisha might be able to coach Jordy to a win, but what will his friends think about Jordy getting advice from a girl?

Icebreaker
By Steven Barwin

Greg Stokes can tell you exactly when his life took a turn for the worse. It was the day he and his new stepsister, Amy, joined the same hockey team. Like it wasn't bad enough sharing a house, school, and friends —

now they're playing on the same line! Before long, the stepsiblings' game is affected by the deep chill between them. Can they thaw their icy relationship for the sake of the team and their new family?

Foul Play
By Beverly Scudamore

When her team's chance at winning the Kicks Soccer Tournament seem to be foiled by holes in their practice field, Remy gets suspicious. Is someone trying to sabotage their chances at winning? She'll bet everything that it's captain of the rival team and ex-best friend Alison who's behind it.

Soccer Star
By Jacqueline Guest

Like her Inuit ancestors, Sam has spent her whole life moving from place to place. But instead of crossing the frozen Arctic in search of food, she's been moving across Canada from military base to military base. Now Sam's left feeling like she doesn't know who she really is or where she belongs. In order to "find herself," Sam has a habit of signing up for too many activities at once. But she refuses to give up either soccer or the school play. Can Sam be a star at both?

Suspended
By Robert Rayner

There's a new principal at Brunswick Valley school, and the establishment is out to shut down the soccer team. One by one the players get suspended from the team. For team captain Shay Sutton, the only way to fight fire is with fire, and he enlists the aid of two high school thugs to help them out.

Check out these Girl's Basketball stories from Lorimer's Sports Stories series

Queen of the Court
By Michele Martin Bossley

When Kallana is sent home for wearing "provocative" clothes, her dad signs her up for the basketball team, and she's mortified: she can't dribble, she can't shoot, and the uniforms are just hideous. But as things get worse at home, basketball practice comes to be a welcome relief, and the self-confidence she learns at the free-throw line helps her prepare for the difficult changes she has to face.

Home Court Advantage
By Sandra Diersch

When Debbie is on the basketball court she feels free and alive. But while she's a good player she's also an aggressive one, and her rough tactics get her in trouble more than once. When Debbie learns she's going to be adopted, however, her world is turned upside down—until, that is, she's accused of stealing from a teammate. Now Debbie must face an uphill battle to prove herself to her new parents and to her team.

LORIMER

Courage on the Line
By Cynthia Bates

Amelie has nightmares. She's a talented and well-liked player on her basketball team in Ottawa, but as a tournament game against her old school approaches she seems more and more frightened. Her teammates wonder why she left her last school in the middle of the year, and why she's reluctant to meet her old friends again. Amelie finds she must confront the past, for her own good and for that of the team.

Shooting Star
By Cynthia Bates

Quyen is a basketball star at her Ottawa school until a fight with her coach forces her to find another team, and she's not sure she likes it. Her new teammates are hard to get along with and one of them goes out of her way to make Quyen her enemy. To make things worse, Quyen's parents start acting strangely and she is worried that something terrible is going to happen. In order to help her family, she must confront her family's past in Vietnam in order to find out the truth.